REDEMPTION TRAIL

PETER BRANDVOLD

WOLFPACK
PUBLISHING
— EST 2013 —

WOLFPACK PUBLISHING
— EST 2013 —

Published in the United States by Wolfpack Publishing, Las
Vegas

Wolfpack Publishing
6032 Wheat Penny Avenue
Las Vegas, NV 89122

wolfpackpublishing.com

Paperback ISBN 978-1-64734-228-9
eBook ISBN 978-1-64734-227-2

REDEMPTION TRAIL

Chapter 1

"Any sign o' them wolves on our trail, Yakima?" asked Paul Cahill.

Yakima Henry squatted near the crest of a low ridge, squinting southward along his and his trail partner's back trail. "Not as far as I can tell."

"Don't you have some—I don't know—*Injun sense* about it?"

Yakima chuckled. He'd have taken offense, but he'd been on the trail with Cahill long enough, since they'd both ridden out of Arizona Territory together nearly two weeks ago, after Cahill had bailed them both out of jail, to know the question was an innocent one.

He shook his head. "Nope, I sure don't, Paul. That's the trouble with bein' only half, I reckon."

Cahill shook his head. "Nasty luck. So you get all the prejudice directed at a red man but little of his—oh, I don't know—*elemental intuition.*"

"I reckon you could say I'm just a tad too far from the tom-toms," Yakima said, chuckling and looking over his shoulder at the older man standing maybe thirty feet down the ridge. "But I do have an *elemental intuition* that's it's nigh on six o'clock and time for grub an' firewater, maybe a little two-handed stud. And I also know if I can pull you out of your mattress sack early enough tomorrow morning and we can hit the trail before noon, we'll be in Denver and at a hurdy-gurdy house by the weekend!"

The big half-breed dropped to hands and knees and crabbed backward down the hill. When he was clear of the ridge, he rose to his full six-feet-four inches, brushed his hands together, shook his long, black hair back from his severely chiseled, copper-skinned face and strode down to where Cahill stood holding the reins of his mule.

"Time to start lookin' for a place to bivouac for the night," he said.

Cahill stood looking up at him, having to tip his head back since he was a whole head shorter than Yakima. A third as wide, as well. Damn near a hundred pounds lighter. He was an older man, mid-sixties, hawk-faced, spindly-framed in a shabby suit and an opera hat, which accentuated his air of learned eccentricity. He reminded Yakima of an educated pauper. He wore his long, unwashed hair in a braid woven with rawhide.

"I didn't mean to offend you, Yakima. If I did, it's just my damn stupid lips flappin' of their own accord, unhooked-up, as they are, to my brain."

"What're you talkin' about, Paul? You still got all your teeth, don't you?"

"No." Cahill pooched out his lips inside his scraggly gray beard and shook his head. "Only about half."

"Well, you didn't lose 'em on my account." Yakima smiled and gave his friend's thin shoulder an affectionate swat. "Come on—let's get mounted. I'm tired an' hungry."

**

They set up camp an hour later on the side of a dike shaped like a dinosaur spine and strewn with rocks. Cactus and cedars offered ample cover from would-be interlopers, like the men on their backtrail. A small stream meandered a quarter mile south of the ridge, likely a tributary of the Arkansas River, probably the Huerfano. The Arkansas passed not far from here, near the town of Pueblo.

When they'd laid their gear out in a small clearing among the rocks, Yakima grabbed up the reins of his black stallion, Wolf and Cahill's mule, which Paul called Ol' Angus with deep affection and said, "I'm gonna take these animals down to the stream for water. Why don't you build a fire, Paul?"

Cahill was on one knee, pulling grub out of a canvas sack. He glanced at Yakima skeptically. "You sure?" He cast his wary gaze to their backtrail. "What about them wolves on our trail?"

The day before yesterday he and Yakima had spied sign of shadowers. Just a glimpse here and there of a horse and rider sky-lined atop a ridge or a telltale curl of distant dust. The trail partners had probably picked up the stalkers in Trinidad, for that's where Yakima and Cahill had holed up for a couple of days, resting their mounts, drinking, gambling and whoring and Cahill had made the mistake of flashing his well-padded money belt.

The old man couldn't help flaunting his wealth. As he'd explained to Yakima, he'd been a poor man—a self-proclaimed "itinerant geologist and mining engineer," which were just high-dollar words for a prospecting desert rat—for most of his adult life. This was on the heels of an expensive education in a fancy college back east funded by a once-rich family from Boston, where he'd read the classics and caught the bug for romantic adventure.

His ship had finally come in a year ago when he'd sold several mining claims to a Mexican conglomerate that had been buying up all the mineral rights in the area, in the Whetstone Mountains, which was where several years ago he'd been scalped by Chiricahua Apaches. His mines might have had some color in them, but they'd needed younger men in better shape than him to dig it out.

As he'd explained to Yakima, this was the first time in the past thirty years he'd had more money than he needed to survive the next few days. At long last, he felt like a rich, proud man, indeed.

And when a rich, proud man is on death's doorstep—Cahill had confessed to Yakima of having a bellyful of cancer—he has a hard time not stomping a little with his tail up. Paul must have flashed that money belt, fat as well-fed diamondback, to one too many tongue-flapping doxies.

Thus, those ominous mares' tails of dust lifting on his and Yakima's backtrail.

Yakima followed the man's gaze out across the vastness of the southern Colorado landscape. Distant mountain ranges humped up in the south and west, some peaks tipped with the ermine of fresh snow—a harbinger of the winter soon to come and all touched with the ochres and salmons of the west-falling sun. Returning his gaze to his friend and seeing the silent, subtle hope in the dying man's eyes, he shrugged.

"Plenty of cover here," he said. "Just keep it small an' we should be all right."

Cahill smiled, relieved. His withering body grew cold at night, after the sun went down, and it yearned for the heat of a dancing fire. Yakima knew this to be true not because of anything the man had said but because he'd seen Paul shivering in a tight ball on warm nights in northern Arizona. His heart had gone out to the loquacious, eccentric man, whom he'd met when they'd both woken up in the same Flagstaff jail together, reeking of cheap perfume and with their heads splitting from too much who-hit-John.

Improbably, they'd become fast friends.

Cahill had paid his as well as Yakima's bail and Yakima had agreed to repay the man by accompanying him to Denver, where Paul intended to catch a train heading north to the Dakota Territory. He'd mentioned a son he wanted to see one last time. The old man had spent so many years in the Southwestern deserts and was by nature flighty and impractical and without a good sense of direction, that he was afraid that once he left the desert without a good trail guide, he'd get hopelessly lost. The only maps he was accustomed to reading were those scribbled by fellow desert rats on the margins of old newspapers or the inside back covers of dime novels.

At least, that's what he'd claimed. Yakima knew what the old, dying man really wanted was companionship and, because of the money belt, protection from would-be predators—animal as well as human.

Yakima had obliged him not only in repayment of the

bail money. After enduring a trying year as the marshal of a small but trouble-plagued town in the Chiricahua Mountains in the southeastern corner of Arizona and with two beautiful young women he was trying to cleanse from his brain—sisters, no less—he felt himself gravitating toward male companionship as he, too, drifted to wherever the fates would take him. After all, whether by choice or the circumstances of his mixed blood heritage, he'd spent most of his life alone.

Despite his taciturn nature, he found it sometimes comforting to wish someone good-night and have the favor returned.

Yakima led his stallion and Ol' Angus down to the stream, which was a good quarter mile from the camp. He let them draw water to their heart's content then led them back to the bivouac in the rocks along the ridge. In his primal hunger for heat, Paul had overbuilt the fire. When the older man wasn't looking, Yakima quietly kicked dirt on a one of the largest logs. He wanted the man to be warm, but if the trail wolves saw the fire, he and Yakima would both likely get a nasty case of lead poisoning.

Paul cooked beans and fatback. Yakima whipped up some tasty baking powder biscuits and brewed coffee though he drank green tea whenever he could find it. He'd acquired the taste for tea back when, fresh out of the frontier army, he'd laid rails for the railroad and had become friends with another eccentric loner, a former Shaolin monk who'd called himself Ralph because no Western folks could pronounce his real handle.

Ralph had brewed green tea every morning and several times a day, insisting it sharpened the senses and heightened perception. When Yakima had given it a try, he'd experienced a similar affect, so he laid in a tin whenever he could find it, which wasn't often.

From Ralph, Yakima had also learned several Eastern fighting techniques, including a few handy, dance-like fighting moves with his feet. Fighting-wise, he'd become almost as good with his feet as with his fists, a necessary advantage for a half-breed loner in the frontier West—especially one with a fiery temper.

Ralph had also gifted his half-breed friend with a beautiful and new (at the time) Winchester '73 Yellowboy repeating rifle. Being a pacifist, Ralph had had no use for guns. Even if he'd had one, he likely wouldn't have used a gun against the men who'd beaten and hanged him after discovering he'd cheated them at poker one drunken Saturday night at a particularly rowdy Hell-on-Wheels encampment.

Now, after the beans, fatback and biscuits had been consumed and the dishes cleaned and put away, Yakima sat a way off from the fire to save his night vision, sipping a second cup of coffee—this one spiced with who-hit-

John. He watched Paul sitting nearer the fire and with a wool blanket pulled up to his shoulders; the older man bobbed his head as sleep assailed him.

Yakima gave a bittersweet smile.

Paul and Ralph. Ralph and Paul. One reminded him of the other though they hailed from two different worlds.

The world could be a funny place that way. Yakima marveled more and more at its vast array of differences as well as its similarities with each passing year. All the sundry, unfathomable curiosities. No life was long enough, allowed a man enough time, to figure even a small percentage of them out. He could only marvel.

Just as Paul's chin nearly touched his chest, he jerked his head up with a start. He caught Yakima staring at him from beyond the fire and flushed a little with chagrin. Chuckling wistfully, he reached into a small canvas rucksack he always kept close to hand. He pulled out a coffee-stained and ash-smeared envelope—the same one he had produced from the rucksack every night as they'd traveled together. And just as on those other nights, he opened the envelope's flap and pulled out three or four sheets of lined notebook paper folded several times and badly wrinkled.

A letter, Yakima speculated. An unfinished one, apparently. Every night, Paul pulled out the letter and then produced a pencil stub from a pocket of his sun-coppered wool vest, licked the tip and went to work by firelight, grumbling and muttering, brows deeply furrowed, scribbling more lines on the crinkled pages. Or maybe he was going over previous lines, changing them, crossing out words, adding others.

Yakima wasn't sure. The old man had never said and Yakima had never asked. He figured if the old man wanted him to know what was on those pages, he'd have told him.

One thing Yakima did know was that the writing of the letter was a chore for Paul. A deeply emotional one. A few times, Yakima had glanced across the fire to see the man sheepishly brushing tears from his craggy, bearded cheeks, sniffing and shaking his head. At those times, Yakima had always quickly looked away, wanting to give the man his privacy.

When Yakima had finished his coffee, he rose, stretched and said, "I'm gonna take the stock down for another drink, take a look around."

Paul kept scribbling on the pages, immersed in his work.

"Keep your rifle close," Yakima advised, glancing at the old Spencer leaning against a rock near Cahill's right elbow. "Any sign of trouble, give a yell. I won't be far."

"Mmhmm," was all the man said. He looked at Yakima, smiled, winked, then took another quick sip of whiskey-laced coffee from his cup and hunkered back over his work, canting the pages to the firelight.

Yakima led the horse and the mule down the slope through the rocks.

He moved slowly, making little noise, glad there was no moon tonight. Still, stars were sprinkled liberally across the firmament. He kept his right gloved hand around the Yellowboy's brass breech, so no reflection would give him away.

He heard nothing but distant coyotes and the vagrant night breeze pushing over and whistling between the rocks and spidery desert brush. Halfway down the slope, he dropped into an arroyo and enjoyed the concealment of the sharply cut banks as he continued leading the two mounts down the decline.

He came to the shallow cut through which the narrow stream murmured, starlight making it shine like a writhing black snake in the darkness. He led the horse and the mule into the stream and dropped their hackamore reins so they could drink freely. He crossed to the stream's far side and, rifle resting on his shoulder, stood looking around and listening.

He wondered where the trail wolves were camped. If they were near, he could spy no fire.

What he'd told Paul about having no "Injun sense" had been a lie. Or at least half a lie. No man who'd been hunted as many times as Yakima had, running from enemies of one stripe or another for most of his life, did not acquire an elemental awareness of his surroundings and an extra sense especially attuned to trouble.

Now that elemental awareness and extra sense had the hair on the back of his neck prickling.

Why?

Were the wolves moving soundlessly around him, surrounding him?

Suddenly, a light shimmered off a separate fork in the stream ahead of him, where it ran along the base of the opposite bank. The shimmering was the deep red of the setting sun. It grew quickly, pulsating.

Yakima's blood warmed. What the hell? The sun had long since set.

Realizing where it was coming from, he whipped around and stared back up the dark incline toward his and Paul's bivouac. The fire shone clearly through the gaps between the rocks, sparking like its own small sun. Paul had tossed too many dry branches on the blaze!

"No, no, no," Yakima muttered, shaking his head. "If they're out here, they'll—"

The unmistakable crack of a rifle shot across the silent night, shattering it.

Paul gave a harrowing cry.

Yakima ran.

Chapter 2

Yakima ran nearly straight up the side of the dike, avoiding the arroyo.

The footing was terrible. He tripped several times, fell, rolled, leaped to his feet and resumed running.

Men were bunched in the rocks between him and Paul. The blades of orange flames showed their positions. Those blades switched positions as the shooters quickly moved up the slope, wending around the rocks, heading for the bivouac.

Paul returned fire from above, his own stabbing orange flames marking his position at the near edge of the bivouac.

Yakima wanted to stop and fire at Cahill's attackers, but he had little chance of hitting a target from his position, with so many rocks and brush clumps between himself and his old friend. He kept running, narrowing the gap between himself and the stalkers.

Above him, amidst the rataplan of rifle fire, Paul yelped.

A man whooped.

Another man shouted, "*Where's the breed?*"

The shout had come from just ahead of Yakima now as he ran. He ran left around a small boulder and saw the outline of the hatted figure crouched on the slope ahead of him, starlight winking off the rifle he cradled in his arms.

"Right here."

The man whipped around. Starlight shone in his widening eyes.

The Winchester leaped and roared in Yakima's hands. Flames bayoneted the man in the chest. The man screamed and flew backward, tossing his rifle into the air, his shirt on fire.

Two more figures shone in the darkness nearly straight ahead of Yakima, fifteen to thirty feet up the slope, nearly to its crest. Both men stopped and turned toward him, one shouting, "Hey, what the…?"

The other said, "Must be the breed!"

Yakima had taken two more strides forward, up the slope. Now he dropped to a knee, pumped a fresh cartridge into the Yellowboy's action, snapped the gun to his shoulder and fired. He pumped and fired again quickly. Each bullet hit its target, the man nearest Yakima getting punched back off his feet before he could take a shot.

The second man, a little farther up the slope and to Yakima's right, sent a round curling the air just off Yakima's left ear half a wink before Yakima's bullet evoked a yelp from the man as it drilled through his breastbone and hurled him backward. He struck on the upslope, bounced off a rock and rolled silently straight down the decline before piling up at the base of a boulder with a wicked-sounding smack.

Yakima pumped a fresh cartridge into the Winchester's breech and slid the barrel from right to left and back again, looking for movement in the darkness before him. Seeing nothing, he rose and took one step before a menacingly low voice said behind him: "Hold it, half-breed."

Yakima froze.

Behind him, he heard a boot come down on gravel. Just as he heard the click of a gun hammer cocking, he crouched, funneling every ounce of his strength and athleticism into his hips and shoulders. He spun lightning-quick, swinging up his left, moccasin-clad foot and thrusting it straight back behind him. Just as he glimpsed the silhouetted head of the man behind him, his left heel smashed into the man's left cheek.

The man grunted shrilly as the savage kick hurled him to his right. The revolver in his hand barked and flashed, the bullet buzzing through the air where Yakima's lower spine had been a half a second earlier but where now, since he was standing two feet left of where he'd been, facing the downslope, his feet widely spread, there was only air. As the man struck the ground with a second grunt, Yakima aimed his Winchester straight out from his right shoulder and pumped two more rounds into the son of a bitch.

The man grunted a third time, rolled once, brush crackling and gravel grinding beneath him, and flopped still.

Yakima wheeled to face the upslope, took a knee again, and looked around, aiming the Winchester again from his shoulder. Again, he watched for a target while keeping his ears pricked for trouble behind him again, as well.

Damn foolish, getting flanked like that.

Around him, nothing moved. The night was deathly silent. Even the coyotes had fallen quiet. The breeze had dropped. The air was still, rich with portent.

The fire glowed in the rocks nearly straight up the rise, fifty feet away. Yakima could see the flames in the gaps between the rocks, but he could not see Paul.

Finally, rising and striding forward, heading toward the fire, he called, "Paul?"

"Here!" came the man's strangled reply somewhere up near where the fire glowed in the rocks, darkly silhouetting the stones in front of it.

"Any more of them?" Yakima asked, quickening his pace but keeping his rifle butt snugged to his shoulder and looking around him, including behind.

Paul did not respond. As Yakima gained the rock-studded bivouac in which the fire's glow had faded a little from its earlier blaze, he kicked something yielding. He looked down, aiming the Winchester down, as well. In the fire's glow, he saw a man's body clad in a long tan duster. It wasn't Paul. The man was bald; a cream slouch hat with a feather in its band lay to one side. The man stared up glassily at Yakima, his mouth nearly wide open as though in astonishment of his unlikely demise.

Yakima had figured there'd been around five men on his and Paul's trail. The occasional dust plumes had told him that. If there'd been five, this man should be the last of them.

Still, he kept his guard up, his eyes skinned.

Again, he called his friend's name.

Seconds passed, and then came the weak reply: "Here."

It had come from Yakima's right. He hurried in that direction then stopped when he saw another man lying between two rocks at the edge of the bivouac. It was Paul. He lay belly down, left cheek pressed against the ground. His right hand was on the Spencer repeating rifle lying beside him.

Yakima dropped to a knee, placed a hand on his

friend's shoulder. "How bad?"

"Bad," Paul said, his voice toneless, breathless.

"Where?"

"Chest."

"I'm gonna roll you over."

Paul looked up at Yakima. "Easy!"

Yakima placed his left hand on the man's shoulder. Cahill sucked a sharp breath as Yakima eased him onto his back. Seeing the dark blood glistening in the light from the fire, on the man's upper right breast, Yakima winced.

The blood was frothy. If hadn't pierced a lung, it had at least nicked it.

Paul looked down at the wound. "Don't look good, does it?"

"I need to get you over to the fire so I can get a better look at it. Can you stand or should I drag you?"

"No, don't drag me!" Paul's voice was pitched with beseeching. "I think…I think I can stand…"

He thrust a hand up to Yakima, who took it, and gently pulled. It took several tries, pulling on Paul's hand and wrapping his other arm around his friend's waist to support him, to get him into a half-standing position. Yakima had to hold his friend up or he would have fallen. He was shaking like a leaf in a strong wind. He seemed to have no strength in his legs.

Slowly, as gently as possible, Yakima half-carried, half-led the man back through the gap between the rocks and over to the fire. He eased him down against his saddle.

"Lay back," Yakima said, pulling a handkerchief out of a back pocket of his buckskin trousers. "I need to get the bleeding stopped."

He wadded the handkerchief then pressed it, gently at first, against the wound from which frothy blood flowed freely. As he increased the pressure, Paul groaned. "Ah, God! Oh, hell, that hurts like the blazes!"

"I have to get the bleeding stopped, Paul."

Cahill thrust his left hand toward a canvas war bag. "Whiskey!"

Holding the handkerchief against Paul's wound with his left hand, Yakima reached across the man, leaning far forward, to dip his hand into the war bag. He pulled out the unlabeled bottle, uncorked it with his teeth, spat out the cork and thrust the bottle into his friend's shaking hand.

Paul tipped up the bottle and took three long gulps, the air bubble bouncing back and forth from the bottom to the neck. Paul lowered the bottle, took several deep breaths, then took another three deep gulps.

He pulled the bottle away from his lips and thrust it toward Yakima. There was a gleam in his eye now, a smile on his bearded mouth. "Snort? It cures what ails ya!"

Yakima shook his head. "I'm gonna stay clear till I get

this bleeding stopped."

"You're not gonna get it stopped."

"What?"

"You're not gonna get it stopped. Even if you did, the bullet's still in there. It's in there deep. I can feel the damn thing. I'm a goner."

"No, you're not. I'll dig it out. I've dug plenty of—"

Paul wrapped his hand around Yakima's wrist and looked at him gravely. "I'm finished. I'd never survive you digging around in my chest for that bullet. I'd bleed out, or go into shock, and that'd be the end of me." He placed his own hand over Yakima's hand holding the sodden handkerchief against the wound, and shook the bottle. "Have a drink with me. I got some unfinished business I need to talk to you about."

"I'm not gonna have a—"

"Take your hand away, dammit! Stop actin' like an old woman. I'll hold the hanky over my own damn wound!" Again, he held Yakima's gaze with his own. He smiled, winked.

Yakima took his hand away from the man's chest. He sank back on his butt, raised his knees and picked up the bottle. His guts were drawn tight as piano wire.

He did not want the man to die. But that's what was going to happen no matter how much he didn't want it to. He hadn't felt so helpless since Faith had died in his arms in Colorado despite every ounce of his being not wanting her to.

"Goddamnit!" he said, and took a pull from the bottle.

"It was my own damn fault. I built up the fire too much. Didn't realize what I was doin'. I just feel so damn cold all the time!"

"I shouldn't have left you."

"They'd have hit us in the morning or maybe tomorrow night." Paul shook his head. "Anyway, what's done is done."

Yakima gazed back at him. He had a hard time keeping tears from his eyes. His throat had grown a hickory knot. "I've enjoyed your company, Paul."

"I've enjoyed yours, too, Yakima. I'm sorry to let you down like this." Paul shook his head and looked down at the wound again, wincing. "Lousy damn luck."

"You sure I can't dig it out?"

"I'm sure." Paul paused, studying Yakima closely, one eye narrowed. "I got a favor to ask you. A big one. I got no right to ask you, and you sure as hell shouldn't feel like you gotta oblige me. But I would appreciate it if you'd at least consider it."

"Anything."

Paul chuckled as he extended his hand for the bottle. "I haven't told you what it is yet."

Yakima thrust the bottle into his friend's shaking

hand. "Don't matter. I'll do it. You got me out of jail, you old scudder." Also, in a short time, Paul had become a good friend. Yakima didn't have many of those. He'd be damned if he didn't feel a tear on his cheek. He was not normally given to displays of emotion. What was happening to him?

Flushing with chagrin, he cursed and brushed away the tear. Paul had seen it, though. He smiled as he lifted the bottle to his lips.

Paul took another big gulp of the whiskey, brushed his sleeve across his mouth and handed the bottle back to Yakima, who took another deep pull himself. With his free hand, Paul picked up the strewn, smudged, penciled pages he'd been scribbling on when Yakima had left the camp to water the stock. He held them up and waved them.

"This is a letter to my son. He's in Dakota Territory. Till last summer, he was stationed at Fort Abercrombie along the Red River of the North. He has a wife—a Sioux woman and four kids. Last summer, he mustered out of the army and homesteaded near the fort. He's also fort sutler—runs a little general store and brewery at the edge of the compound. Him an' me—Paul, Jr.—got crossways years ago. After I left his mother and lit out for the desert."

Cahill held up the letter. A sheen of emotion shone in his eyes, which turned red around the edges. "This here is a confession of all my sins in hopes my boy'll forgive me. Or at least understand who I am…er, *was*…an' why I did what I did. It's by no means an excuse. It's a confession of my sins and it's a pronouncement of my love for him and my grandchildren. I want him to read it. I could put it in the mail, but I want him to have the money belt, too."

Paul shook his head. "I wouldn't trust the mail with that letter nor with the belt. The belt's got a little over five thousand dollars in it. I want Paul to have it. He has him a poor little farm and too many mouths to feed and there's been a drought up there for the past several years. I hear about him through a friend of mine, an officer stationed up there. We went to school together back east—Wes Hewitt an' me. For the past several years, he's kept me up to date on my son's life."

Paul made a sour expression and shook his head. "He's had a hard life, the boy has. Don't sound like it's gettin' much better."

Paul took another deep pull from the bottle, swallowed. Tears were rolling freely down his cheeks, glistening in his beard in the firelight. "I always wanted to make the trek up there to see him…ask him to forgive this old reprobate of a father for his many sundry sins. I don't know—I reckon I figured I had all the time in the world. Wasn't too worried about it." He drew a deep breath, shook his head. "Not till the sawbones in Tucson told me I was full of cancer."

He turned to Yakima. "I know it's gettin' late in the year. I know it's Dakota Territory. I know I have no right to ask you to make such a long trip for me, but…"

"Sure, Paul…"

"I'll buy you a train ticket, give you extra for your trouble."

"Don't want neither. Wolf and I can make it up there and back faster than any damn train. Hate the contraptions, an' they don't much like me, neither."

"It'd be faster."

"The way we travel—cross-country and hell-for-leather?"

"Dammit," Paul sobbed, giving a soft, strangling wail, "I do love my boy an' miss him an' regret not having watched him grow up. I regret how I treated him and his mother. And I sure wish you'd give him these two things in person and talk a little to him about me, face to face. Man to man, since you're the only friend I got."

He scrubbed tears from his cheeks with both hands, streaking his beard with blood from his chest. "Tell him how I was at the end—a good man, more or less. A man who truly did love his son and regretted how I treated him and his ma."

Yakima had scuttled over to sit close beside his friend. He snaked an arm around the sobbing man's thin shoulders and cleared his throat though there was no way to clear that damn, tight knot. His own voice quaking a little, he said, "You got it. I will deliver the letter and the money. You rest easy, drink your whiskey, an'…"

He let his voice trail off as Paul's body jerked and fell slack. He looked down at his friend. Paul sagged to one side in Yakima's arm, his eyes closed.

He was gone.

Chapter 3

Yakima stared at the old man's body slumped against his arm.

He felt wretched. Hollowed out. Empty.

He hadn't felt so miserable since Faith had died, leaving him alone and feeling even more alone than he'd been before she'd entered his life. He felt even more alone now than after he'd left Apache Springs in the Chiricahuas and had started drifting north, before he'd met Paul in that jail cell in Tucson.

A grunt sounded from out beyond the sphere of diminished firelight, from the direction of the slope. There was a brief clatter of rocks.

Heart thudding heavily, burning with fury in his chest, Yakima eased Paul to the ground. He rose and grabbed his Yellowboy. He quickly loaded the rifle from his shell belt and jacked a round into the chamber.

Jaws set hard, he walked out through the rocks and stopped just beyond them where the slope dropped darkly down away from him, spotted with pale rocks and shadowy clusters of brush. He looked around.

A shadow moved low to the ground on his left.

There must have been more than five trail wolves, after all. Paul must have accounted for two of them. One man he must have wounded but not killed. The man was crawling down the slope very slowly, grunting and groaning quietly with the effort.

Yakima headed that way, stepping over rocks and tufts of brush and cactus.

As he approached the crawling man, the man stopped suddenly. He lay belly down to the ground, hands flat against the ground to either side of him. He turned his head slowly to gaze up at Yakima, dread in his night-cloaked features.

He was a large, fat, round-faced man. Bearded and nearly bald. Yakima remembered seeing him in the Rocky Mountain Club in Trinidad, when he and Paul had been there, drinking and playing craps and twenty-one.

Yakima could smell the sweat and blood on him now.

Yakima tightened the rifle in his hands.

"No," the man choked out. "Please…"

Yakima's heart thudded in fury. Rage burned in his bowels.

He drew a deep breath, raised the Yellowboy, aimed carefully and shot the man in the head.

He ejected the spent cartridge, seated a fresh round and shot the man again.

He ejected the spent cartridge, seated fresh and fired again.

Again…

And again.

In his mind, he was not just shooting the man on the ground before him. He was again killing every man in the pack who'd killed Paul.

When he'd emptied the Yellowboy, he unholstered the stag-gripped .44 from the holster thonged low on his right leg. He fired until the wheel was empty, until the human predator responsible for Paul's death was a bleeding mass of dead flesh on the ground before him.

***

Yakima knew he wouldn't sleep, so, after running down his horse and Ol' Angus and returning both animals to the camp, he didn't even try.

He left the stalkers where they lay. The predators could have the wolves who'd killed Paul. As for Paul, Yakima wrapped the man for burial in Paul's own bedroll. Though Paul had given up the prospecting trade, he had not given up all the implements of his former profession. He'd still carried a pick and a shovel strapped to his saddle.

Using both, Yakima went to work digging a grave at the edge of the bivouac. He kept the fire small. He didn't need it either for warmth or to see by; he kept it burning as a nod to dead friend, who lay beside it, wrapped in his red-striped gray blanket roll. Paul had been cold long enough. Soon, he'd be colder. Yakima might as well keep him warm for as long as he could.

The rising sun found him barebacked and sweating from the strenuous labor, setting the last few rocks on the freshly mounded grave and erecting a cross he'd fashioned from two relatively straight cottonwood branches and rawhide. When he'd planted the cross at the head of the grave, he stepped back.

Staring down at the fresh grave marked with the cross, a fresh wave of sorrow swept through him. His guts churned and loneliness settled heavily on his shoulders.

Maybe Yakima's own time would come soon. An end to the struggle. However, it couldn't come before he'd taken Paul's money belt and letter to his son in Dakota Territory.

Yakima Henry was a man who kept his promises.

He donned his calico shirt and necklace of grizzly claws taken from a grizzly he'd killed before the beast, try as it had, had been able do the same to him. He went through Paul's grub sack and gear, kept what little he needed and left the rest, including Paul's saddle and bridle, in a pile near the grave. Maybe some fellow wayfarer would stumble on the utensils and find a use for them.

For sentimental reasons that filled him with a wry chagrin, Yakima decided to hold onto the mule. The mule would come in handy for packing the extra supplies required for the long trek to Dakota.

At least, that's why he told himself he'd keep the mule though deep down he knew he wanted to hold onto ol' Angus because it was like holding on to a part of Paul himself. On lonely night camps, the mule would remind him of Paul's congenial companionship and eccentric, self-deprecating humor.

Even of the many ways he'd always cheated at cards.

Chuckling, Yakima fastened the money belt around his waist and stowed the letter in his saddlebags. He did not read the letter nor had any intention of doing so. If Paul had wanted him to know what was in it, he'd have let him read it. What was in that letter would remain between Paul and his son.

The sun was just clearing the horizon when Yakima swung up onto Wolf's back. He peered through the rocks at the dead men strewn across the slope below and to either side. Buzzards swirled in several flocks over the slope, barking and quarreling on the slope itself, fighting over the carrion. They and the smell of fresh blood were making Wolf and Ol' Angus nervous. Since Yakima had retrieved the beasts, the mule had given frequent, edgy brays while the stallion whickered, nose turned to the downslope, tail arched, ears pricked.

"Rest easy, pard," Yakima said, patting the horse's left wither with the hand holding the mule's reins. "We're just now leavin' this bone orchard, damn them to hell, anyway!"

He swung the horse around, touched the heels of his moccasins to Wolf's flanks and, leading the mule by its bridle reins, headed through the rocks and up the ridge, quickly cresting it then starting down the other side.

Two days later, he rode into the sprawling city that the old cow town of Denver had become in only the past few years. He entered the town askance, riding around the fawn prairie and coming in through Auraria, a smaller town than Denver had become, on the south side of the confluence of Cherry Creek and the South Platte River.

It was quieter over here, with fewer people, meaning there was less chance of him being noticed by one of the bounty hunters he knew were keeping an eye out for him, since his likeness had been sketched on several wanted circulars over the past several years. Some of the men he'd killed defending himself or others had been important men and/or lawmen, thus there were several federal warrants floating around boasting high-figure bounties.

One of the so-called "important" men he'd killed had been the old pimp and killer, Bill Thornton, who'd murdered Faith. Killing Thornton, who'd had connections in high places in Colorado Territory, had caused federal men to dog Yakima's trail. Some of those federal men he'd killed had upped the ante on his head.

Maybe it was stupid to have risked entering Denver instead of riding wide around it, but he'd need to lay in supplies for the journey north. Maybe more importantly, his trek up from that bloody, rocky slope where he'd buried Paul had been a lonely, brooding one, indeed. Grieving Paul had made him grieve Faith, as well, and then he'd lamented his own sour luck in general. After two days of sawing away on his own heart strings, he felt as though a dark cloud as large as the whole territory was hovering low and keeping stride with him, Wolf and Ol' Angus.

At times like this, when he was feeling small and down on his luck and lonely and angry and downright mean and sick at heart, there was really only one thing that could make him feel better. Well, two things. In order of importance, they were:

A woman and whiskey.

He knew just the place and just the gal to pull his head out of his own hind end. He was headed that way, riding through Denver proper now and looking around and marveling at all the foot and wheel traffic, including horse-drawn rail cars, around him.

Good Lord—look at all the fancily tricked out carriages and the high fashions of the men and women hustling along Broadway! Yakima was astonished by the number of new buildings that had gone up since his last visit— some great big brick or masonry buildings including a jaw-droppingly vast complex called the Tabor Opera House on the corner of Sixteenth and Curtis Streets. Yakima had once paged through a book showing pictures of castles in Europe and other such places across the ocean, and if this building didn't look every bit as grand as the grandest of those, why, he'd boil his left boot and eat it!

He stopped Wolf and Ol' Angus just north of the opera house to gawk, hang-jawed, at a big hotel that had been erected on the street opposite the opera house. The hotel, called the *La Grande Parai*, vied only with the Tabor Opera House for opulence. What attracted Yakima's attention next was a whole bevy of grandly dressed folks just then stepping out through the hotel's large, brass-and-glass doors and, talking loudly in what sounded like a foreign tongue, the women tittering and men laughing importantly, throwing their gaudy faux-western hats and immaculately coifed heads back and showing their full sets of supremely white teeth.

There must have been a good twenty or thirty in the party, all decked out like characters from one of Buffalo Bill's Wild West Shows—even the women, of which there were at least a dozen and not a plain-faced one in the lot. Dressed in lace-trimmed velvet gowns, flamboyant hats, diamond-studded chokers and adorned with a profusion of gaudy jewelry—as well as revealing more than a good bit of creamy white skin—they were headed for a string of carriages the likes of which Yakima had never seen before, either.

The wheeled contraptions shone like jewels there in front of the hotel, with their sleek designs and cherry panels and brass fittings including brass oil lamps and air horns. They had real glass windows framed with tied-back red or green velvet drapes, not just square holes covered with deer skin curtains, which Yakima was more accustomed to. Even the doors had glass windows, and they were tricked out with brass handles and brass shields on their lower panels.

The horses were all blooded and, hitched to one carriage, they were all black. Hitched to another they were all white. Hitched to the third, they were all blue roans with nearly identical shading.

"Say, there—what are you looking at?"

Yakima had been so busy marveling at the carriages and the men and women filing into them, the men obviously carrying rifles in leather or buckskin sheaths—likely sporting rifles—that he had a hard time switching his gaze to the man trotting toward him astride a fine black Morgan. Beneath Yakima, Wolf whickered and shifted his weight, apparently sensing danger.

Yakima didn't see anything dangerous about the man riding toward him and now drawing rein within ten feet of him. In fact, the man was attired so bizarrely in a snow-white buckskin coat and fancily embroidered and fringed snow-white buckskin pants and a broad-brimmed hat as large-around as any sombrero Yakima had ever seen anywhere even in Mexico, that the half-breed had to stifle a laugh.

"Say, there! Say, there!" the man on the Morgan repeated, a stylish pair of pewter-framed spectacles mounted on the bridge of his long, pale nose set above a thick, deep-red, handlebar mustache with upswept and waxed ends. "What are you gawking at?"

Yakima just realized that in fact the opulently clad party hadn't been speaking in a foreign tongue. It had just sounded foreign to his ears, because it was so elaborately accented. Irish, Yakima guessed on the fly. He'd worked with many Irishmen on the transcontinental railroad, though those men had been considerably less outlandishly attired than the pilgrim sitting before him now. And while the accents had been similar, theirs hadn't been nearly as emphasized, nor as loud except on Friday and Saturday Nights at Hell on Wheels.

Taken off-guard not only by the man before him, but everything he'd seen in the past ten gawking minutes, Yakima merely chuckled, still amused by the man's appearance, and shrugged his heavy shoulders. "What's that, amigo?"

"I know what you're staring at, you damn savage!"

That wiped the smile off Yakima's broad, severely chiseled face almost immediately. The man before him jerked his head toward one of the three carriages—the one to which the cream horses had been hitched. Apparently, that carriage had been reserved for the ladies in the party. Now a good six or seven of them had turned to peer through the glass windows at Yakima. They were either bunched in front of the windows or clumped in the open door, the ones in back looking over and around the ones in front.

The women stared in wide-eyed wonder at the big, copper-skinned half-breed sitting the fine black stallion and holding the reins of the mule. Yakima supposed they were regarding him in similar fashion to the way he'd been gawking at *them*. Well, not *at* them directly, but at the hotel and the carriages and the horses and the men and the whole kit 'n' kaboodle!

The expression on the face of the man before him,

though, told Yakima the man had misunderstood the nature of Yakima's stare.

"Oh, no," Yakima said, returning the smile to his face despite the epithet that the Brit had spat at him and which would get most men their hats—and possibly several teeth—handed to them. "No, no, I...wasn't, uh..."

A couple of the garishly attired women in the carriage turned to each other and tittered. One said quietly but loudly enough for Yakima to hear, "...right handsome figure of a man, despite, you know...despite his being..."

"A *savage?*" asked another.

They all laughed devilishly, some covering their mouths with their hands.

The man before Yakima flushed. He hardened his jaws.

"Why are you not on the reservation, you rock-wor-shipping savage?" he wanted to know, spittle flecking his plump red lips beneath the drooping red mustache. "A reservation-jumper, are you? I've heard of your lot!"

Yakima's eyes hardened as he stared back at the man.

A dark, forbidding voice in his head warned, "*Easy, now. Easy, now. This is Denver. This ain't the high an' rocky.*"

His own gut tightened in dread. He knew how many times in the past he'd paid the voice no heed. No heed at all.

And had given the devil the hindmost.

Chapter 4

"What do you have to say for yourself, redskin?" asked the outlandishly costumed man on the sleek Morgan. By now, everyone in the man's party had paused in their revelry to stare in open amusement toward the man confronting the savage. "Go on—what do you have to say about riding into civilized society and gawking at our women?"

He glanced smugly over his shoulder as though to make sure all the others in his group was appreciating the way he was so bravely and thoroughly dressing-down the savage rock-worshipper in the heart of Denver.

Yakima shaped another smile. It did not reach his coal-black eyes.

"What do I have to say for myself?" he said.

"Yes!" the popinjay bellowed for the benefit of his audience, glancing around at them again, sitting straight up in his saddle and puffing out his chest. "What do you have to say for yourself?"

He turned back to Yakima and shaped a supercilious smirk, waiting for the rock worshipper's reply.

Still smiling, Yakima booted Wolf up close to the gent, sitting alongside him, Wolf's head facing the Morgan's tail. The man frowned a little, suddenly puzzled and no longer quite so brave but apparently unwilling to lose face by giving ground.

"Sometimes, friend," Yakima said. "Actions speak louder than words."

With that, he thrusted his face straight toward the man, dropping his chin. He head-butted him soundly. When Yakima pulled his head back, he saw the man's long, fine nose sitting sideways against his face. He looked as though he'd been struck in the face by a ripe tomato. The man's spectacles fell away, both lenses shattered, the frames busted in the middle.

The man jerked his head up and loosed a girlish scream, cupping both hands to his ruined nose.

Every girl and woman in the all-female carriage gasped and clasped her hand over her nose.

A rumbling rose from among the men.

Yakima calmly donned his hat and unsheathed his stag-butted .44, clicked the hammer back, and aimed it warningly at the men milling in and around the other two carriages. Some of the outlandishly attired gents had begun unsheathing their rifles, but when they saw the copper-skinned savage aiming the hogleg at them, they all froze, eyes growing darker and larger.

The man with the ruined beak screamed again, this time with rage, and, still holding his hand over his bloody nose, shouted toward the other men, "Do you see what this savage to my *nose? Kill* him!"

Keeping the Colt aimed at the men in the party, Yakima calmly booted Wolf around the injured foreigner's horse and continued on his way, swinging the Colt slowly back behind him to keep the men in his sights. That seemed to hold them. They and the women slowly swiveled their heads as they watched the Colt-wielding savage ride on up the street, the mule following and braying in characteristic mule fashion.

"What are you waiting for?" wailed the broken-beaked popinjay, still holding his nose where Yakima had left him. "*Shoot* him!"

Yakima turned Wolf east down the first cross street he came to then, when the foreigners were out of sight, he holstered the Colt and booted Wolf into a spanking trot. He traced a circuitous route through downtown Denver, in case anyone were following, then reined up outside one of the few remaining log structures in Denver proper and which was identified by a big, sun-faded sign painted in red letters across its second story, just above the hayloft doors: SVEN NORGAARD'S ROCKY MOUNTAIN LIVERY & FEED COMPANY.

Two men in overalls and floppy-brimmed hats were just then unloading feed sacks from a weathered green wagon to which two stout donkeys were hitched, and carrying the sacks inside the barn. Sven Norgaard him-self—tall, blond, blue-eyed, and long-limbed—glanced at Yakima then carried a feed sack inside before returning empty-handed and scowling at the big half-breed just then reining up in front of his barn.

The man placed his big, gloved hands on his broad hips, gave his head a rueful shake, smiling fatefully. "Who you runnin' from now, Henry?"

"Hey, Sven," Yakima said after casting a quick glance behind him, to see if he were being shadowed. "Long time no see!"

"Answer the question. Angry father or jealous hus-band?"

"What?" Yakima laughed. "No, no—you got it all wrong." He scowled suddenly, curiously. "Why do you ask?"

"I seen you comin' from a block away and counted the number of times you looked behind." The blond man of obviously Scandinavian descent raised his hands, show-ing seven fingers. "That many." He lowered his hands. "Every time you ride in, you're always lookin' behind you."

"This is a growing town and a fella can't be too careful." Yakima swung his right boot over his saddle horn, dropped straight down to the ground, then, casting another quick glance behind him, led Wolf and Ol' Angus up the wooden ramp past Norgaard and into the concealment of the barn's thick shadows rife with the malty, heady smell of fresh hay, straw, oats, and cracked corn. "That said, if any overdressed popinjays with foreign accents come around, inquiring about the rock-worshippin' savage who turned one of their party's noses sideways, redirect 'em for me, will ya?"

"Oh, Lordy!" Norgaard shook his head, chuckling. "Don't tell me you got crossways with the Earl of Cork his ownself—Sir William Anthony Boyle!"

"I don't know." Yakima grabbed his saddlebags off Wolf's back and slung them over his right shoulder. "Might have. Is this Earl of Cork fellow not quite as tall as me, long of bone and nose, pale as a debutante, fur-eyed, an' dressed purtier'n a ten-dollar whore?"

"That's him!"

Yakima winced. "Then I reckon so."

"Good Lord, man—you sure know how to pick 'em!" It was Norgaard's turn to lean forward and cast a wary gaze up the street in the direction from which Yakima had come. "Nasty as a stick-teased rattlesnake! Has a purty wife, though. I seen 'em when they all got off the train together." He glanced at the other man—short, stocky, and middle-aged—now unloading the feed sacks from the wagon alone—and said, "Earl and me was down at Union Station pickin' up some shoein' iron shipped from Kansas City. The earl's bunch, they was all laughin' an' drinkin' as they got off their own private rail car, but they was beratin' their help like rented mules!"

"Special guests of some senator who owns a mine in Leadville," Earl interjected as he walked past Yakima and Norgaard with a feed sack on his beefy shoulder. "They're headin' up into the Black Hills on a huntin' trip. Even the ladies!" Earl shook his head, indicating how insane he thought the notion of hauling women into southern Dakota was when everyone knew that dangerous white men and even still quite a few dangerous Indians, haunted that country between said brigands' stage and bank holdups, ranch raids and their sundry other travesties against humanity.

"Nasty bunch." Norgaard frowned at Yakima. "How'd you get crossways with 'em?"

"They got crossways with me."

"Ah," the livery owner said, smiling and nodding his understanding. "Well, don't worry—I'll keep your hoss and your, uh…mule, there…" He must have noticed the mule for the first time, and was wondering about it. "I'll keep 'em hid away so no one snoopin' around for you will notice 'em."

"I'd be obliged if you'd tend these mounts good for me, Sven. They gotta get me up to the Dakota Territory. Way up there. I'm talkin the Red River."

"The Red River?" The big blond drew his head back in astonishment. "What in the hell are you headin' up into that savagely—that *savagely cold* country this time of the year. Hell, I come from there—Grand Forks, as a matter of fact and I never wanna step foot up there again. In the summer there's ticks an' mosquitoes not to mention brutal heat and humidity. In the winter, there's—"

"I know all about the winter," Yakima said, holding his hands up, palms out. "After my last winter up there, a few years back, I vowed to both me an' my hoss to never subject us to that kinda cold ever again, but" he sighed, wagged his head in defeat "I promised a friend."

"What kind of a friend would send you to the Red River of the North country this late in the year?"

"A dead one," Yakima said, grimly. He peeked under the flap of the saddlebag pouch hanging down over his chest just to make sure the letter was still tucked inside. He closed the flap and patted the pouch in satisfaction. "Yessir, a dead one. Poor fella. Anyway, Sven, tend the mounts good an' lay in a store of trail supplies for me, will ya? All the usual stuff. An' some green tea if you can find it."

"Anything else?" Norgaard asked, ironically.

"Yeah, one more thing." Yakima smiled. "Is Julia Vangelova still in town?"

As Norgaard led Wolf and the mule deeper into the barn's shadows, he glanced over the horse's back at Yakima, his brows arched. "Julia Vangelova? You dog!" He chuckled. "Has her own parlor house now, don't ya know? Over on Twelfth Street, across from the Western Union office and the old opry house."

"Twelfth Street across from the Western Union office an' the old opry house," Yakima said, nodding slowly, grinning. "All right, then!" He winked.

"You best scrape the shit off your boots before you enter Julia's place. Madam Vangelova runs one of the nattiest places…an' tightest ships…on the Front Range. She's been known to throw men into the alley just for cussin!"

"Madam Vangelova, eh?" Again, Yakima grinned. "I like the sound of that. Thanks, Sven. I'll be back for those cayuses in the mornin' Maybe not too early!"

He winked then, chuckling, tramped on out of the barn and back in the direction from which he'd come, sticking close to the shadows on the street's south side in case any of the earl's men had decided to start their Great Western Hunt by bagging a half-breed on the streets of Denver.

It had been two years since he'd last visited Denver. Much had changed but much had stayed the same, so it took him only fifteen minutes, keeping to the backstreet shadows, to find the parlor house he was looking for. He approached through the break between the Western Union office and the limestone opera house which, while large, was maybe an eighth the size of the new one farther south.

The house facing Yakima, on the street's opposite side, was a three-story clapboard affair. Possibly a saloon at one time, but it had been renovated nicely and painted white with black trim including black rails on the second-story balcony that ran across the entire front of the building. A half-dozen men and young women milled together on the balcony, talking and laughing, one of the girls and one of the men, clad in a three-piece business suit, danced together slowly though there was no music.

All the men were drinking and/or smoking. One of the girls smoked a cigarette protruding from a long, black holder that she seemed to enjoy flourishing as she talked with a very fat older gent, also clad in a three-piece suit.

The first-floor veranda was the same size as the veranda, its floor and rails also painted black. A tastefully small sign hanging from chains beneath the veranda roof, over the four steps leading to the street, read simply: MADAM VANGELOVA. Only one man and one girl, dressed in bright reds and purples and wearing an enormous, floppy-brimmed black hat, sat out there together, facing each other in wicker chairs.

The girl lounged back lazily in her chair, one bare leg hooked over an arm. The man, in his middle thirties, leaned forward, facing her, talking to her with what appeared a serious expression on his pale face beneath a cap of short, curly black hair.

A drummer with a crush on the gal, Yakima told himself with an inaudible snort.

Yakima returned his gaze to the sign.

"Madam Vangelova," he muttered to himself. "Yessir, I like the sound of that."

Obviously, Julia had come far. The last time Yakima had seen her, she'd still been working for percentages down near Union Station, albeit in a somewhat tony if rustic cattleman's club. She'd been one of the most popular girls in the club's remuda and, of course since Yakima was a half-breed and not allowed inside the club, he'd slipped in one night, anyway, ducking through the door between two distracted bouncers then allowing the thick tobacco smoke and his tipped-forward hat to half-ways conceal him.

It had been late and most of the men in the room had been drunk and heavily involved in the pasteboards, roulette wheels, or craps dice, so no one had paid much attention to him until he sat down to a game of twenty-one and the gambler he'd fleeced mercifully had called him out suddenly for a "No-good stinking, cheating savage and what the hell do you think you're doing, mixing in civilized society in the first place, you half-breed cur?"

That had brought Yakima to his feet quicker than a mountain lion ready to pounce. But before he could reach across the table to take a fistful of the gambler's shirt collar and raise his other fist for a skull-crunching punch, the ravishing little brunette with the beguilingly long lashes and slanted, dark-brown eyes, whom he'd been making eyes with for the past two hours, had suddenly leaped into his arms, yelling into his ear above the din of the crowd, "Take me upstairs before you're a dead man, you crazy Indian!"

Seeing two beefy bouncers hustling through the crowd and the gambler plucking a pearl-gripped over-and-under silver-chased derringer from a pocket of his brocade vest and rather enjoying the suppleness of the scantily clad little doxie in his arms—Yakima wheeled and hurried through the tables and the milling crowd for the stairs.

By the time he'd reached the stairs, he'd lost sight of the bouncers and the gambler. By the time he was half-way up the stairs, weaving among the men and girls heading either up or down, the little doxie in his arm was sticking her tongue in his ear, as if to make sure he didn't have a change of heart before reaching the second-story where the cribs were laid out.

Before they'd even reached the girl's room, she'd somehow squirmed out of every article of her clothing which didn't consist of much more than a corset and bustier as well as a pair of high, black stiletto's and was squirming against him like a cat in heat, moaning, "I've never been with a savage before!"

That had been Yakima's introduction to Julia Vangelova, whose parents hailed from somewhere in eastern Europe though she'd been born here in America. Yakima didn't know much, if anything, about eastern European women, but if the rest were tireless spitfires like Julia, he'd bet their men died young.

He hadn't even minded her calling him a savage. She'd played the part rather well, herself.

Chapter 5

After that first night with Julia, Yakima looked her up whenever he was in town, which hadn't been all that many times, but they'd managed to use their time together well.

Now he took a moment to ponder on a strategy for locating her in her new digs. It was too early to waltz in the front door. The crowd inside was likely not large enough nor drunk enough yet not to notice the big, long-haired Injun in buckskins cavorting about the place and there probably wasn't enough smoke nor shadows to conceal him, either. He came up with an alternate plan.

Glancing around to make sure he had no shadowers from the earl's party, he angled to the right of where a half-dozen horses and a red-wheeled chaise stood before the two wrought-iron hitch racks.

He followed a cinder path around behind Madam Vangelova's and walked up to the back door. He tapped once on the upper glass panel then tripped the latch, opened the door and poked his head into a kitchen where a large, buxom black woman was stirring a large pot on a big, black range.

"Uh, pardon me, ma'am," Yakima said, sticking his head in a little farther.

A rumble of conversation and the patter of a piano issued from another room and the pot the black woman was stirring was bubbling loudly. Yakima cleared his throat and called again, a little louder: "Pardon me, ma'am, I have—"

The woman jerked with a start then snapped her head toward Yakima. She gave a shrill scream, dropping the spoon in her hand and, stepping backward, splaying a hand across her opulent bosom clad in a starched black dress and cream apron. "Oh, Lordy!"

Yakima held up a placating hand. "Not to worry. You're not under attack. Western Union across the street sent me." He brushed his thumb across a breast pocket of his buckskin shirt. "I have a message for Madam Vangelova."

"Oh, Lordy!" the black woman exclaimed again. "I turn around an' see a red man in my kitchen!"

"I know," Yakima said. "It's very unsettling. But, like I said, I have a message—"

"She's in her room." The woman stooped to retrieve the spoon. She wiped it off on her apron then pointed it at the ceiling. "Third floor. Last room, very front of the building." She shook her head then returned her attention to the soup, exclaiming once more nearly as loudly as before, "Oh Lordy—I thought for sure the red men were overrunnin' Denver again!"

Yakima strode forward, heading for a closed oak door straight ahead of him.

"Oh, no!" the woman said, her voice sharply admonishing. "That door there. Back stairs. Lordy!"

Yakima glanced at her. He must have looked a little crestfallen; he'd been looking forward to seeing what kind of festivities were occurring out in what, judging by the sounds emanating through the closed oak door, he assumed was the more festive part of the hurdy-gurdy house. Beneath the piano's pattering, he could hear men and women laughing and the clicking of a roulette wheel.

"What?" the black woman said, snapping her eyes wide. "You didn't think you'd be wanted beyond *that* door, did you? Why should you be when I ain't?"

Yakima gave a rueful snort. "Good point." He turned to the door the woman had indicated on his right—a narrow plank door with wainscoting tacked over it and which wobbled on its leather hinges and opened it. A narrow wooden stairway rose into darkness.

Yakima pinched his hat brim to the woman then, leaving the door open a crack so he'd have a little light to navigate by, he climbed the stairs. He passed the second-floor landing and continued to the door at the top. He tripped the latch and stepped into a large, carpeted hall stretching away before him.

A dozen closed doors shone in each wall, as did several oil paintings and a mounted grizzly skull, even a pair of crossed cavalry sabers. The carpet beneath Yakima's boots was thick and lush. It smelled new, not sour like the carpets of the hurdy-gurdy houses he was more accustomed to.

"Yessir," he said softly to himself. "Madam Vangelova has done right well for herself."

As Yakima strode toward the door at the hall's far end, he could hear intimate male and female voices behind a couple of the doors, a couple of girls talking behind another and the groaning of bed springs getting a good working out behind yet another. As he walked, a door just ahead on his left opened and a small, bald man stepped out, carrying a cherry wood, ivory-handled walking stick in one hand, a crisp brown derby hat in the other.

Yakima stopped or he would have run over the little gent, who paused to peer back through the door and to blow a kiss back into the room. "Same time next week, my little bird!" he said.

Unseen to Yakima's eyes, a girl squealed.

The little gentleman chuckled. He drew the door

closed, latching it softly, then, apparently spying Yaki-ma in the corner of his eye, snapped his head around. He peered up, eyes wide in shock, at the big half-breed towering over him. The man scowled, raked his gaze up and down Yakima's big, brawny, buckskin-clad frame, then returned his gaze to Yakima's face, clucked his disapproval and shook his head.

"Good *Lord!* Who're they letting in *now?"*

He wheeled and scampered off toward the mouth of the stairs ten feet beyond, in the middle of the hallway.

"Yeah," Yakima grunted behind him. "I get that a lot."

He continued past the stairs to the door at the end of the hall. His heart quickening in anticipation of his reunion with the beguiling Julia Vangelova, he raised his right hand to knock. He froze. He heard a man speaking on the other side of the door, in tight and angry voice.

"…yeah, don't you worry, you little bitch, I know all about it…"

"Let me go, damn you!" came a woman's own taut, angry plea.

"The rigged gambling wheels," the man continued, his voice tight but vaguely, mockingly sing-song. "The second dealing and the bottom dealing at the twenty-one tables…your pretty little spies…hidden mirrors…the bags under the tables and the sleeve rigs your dealers wear!"

"You're *mad!"*

"Oh and the weighted craps dice and the swivel on the roulette wheel!"

"You are hurting me, Stillwell," the woman complained. "My god…you're…you're strangling…"

"I *will* strangle you, too, Julia," the man said, even tighter and angrier than before, "if you don't play by my rules an…"

The man cut himself off as Yakima, who'd heard enough, opened the door.

The man had Julia leaning forward against a desk on the far side of the room, between two large, lace-curtained windows. The man, dressed like a well-to-do gambler in a black suit, pink shirt, and matching paisley vest, had long, thick red hair curling down from his bowler hat. He pressed his tall, lean body down hard against Julia's, using his weight to hold her fast against the desk.

He had one arm pinned back behind her. His other hand was on the back of her neck, his fingers digging deeply into her skin. Her mass of rich, black hair had come down to partly cover her face, which was turned toward Yakima and hang in a messy tumble off her right shoulder.

As soon as the door had opened, the red-haired man had turned quickly to see Yakima step into what appeared a nicely appointed office with an adjoining parlor area, comfortable furniture arranged around a neat, chrome wood stove to his left.

The man's blue eyes blazed in fury beneath furry red brows, his long, delicately sculpted cheeks reddening above a thick, red mustache. He hardened his jaws and flared his nostrils. "Who in the hell are—"

That's as far as he got.

By then, Julia had wrenched her right hand free of his grip. She swept her hand forward across the desk and grabbed what appeared an obsidian-handled stiletto off the top of a cloth-covered account book near a pink-shaded Tiffany lamp. She took advantage of the man's having eased the pressure on her back to swing her arm around backward in a blur of fast motion, raising the hand with the stiletto in it and burying the blade hilt deep in the side of the man's neck.

The man's eyes snapped wide.

"Oh," he said, as though he'd been given a piece of hard to believe information.

He jerked his head back then stumbled sideways, away from Julia. He turned his head and dropped it slightly, rolling his eyes sideways as though to get a look at the knife sticking out of his neck.

"Oh," he said again, a little more shrilly that time.

He stumbled sideways into a glass-doored bookcase, making the bell lamp on top of it chime and flailed a hand toward the stiletto's obsidian handle. Only a little blood was oozing up around the deeply embedded blade. Only a little, that was, until the man wrapped his hand around the blade and, with a fierce grunt and stretching his lips back from his teeth, pulled it out.

Blood geysered out of the deep wound and severed carotid artery. It splattered across the leather swivel chair facing the desk and onto the desk itself, the dark-red stream missing Julia by inches.

The man lifted his head and wailed, his face suddenly a mask of bald terror. He tried to push himself off the bookcase while trying to clamp one hand over his neck. He didn't make it. He was losing blood and strength fast.

He slid along the window behind him, to his right, tried to take a step forward, then fell to his knees. His bloody hand dropped from his blood-oozing neck to glare up at Julia, who stared down at him in shock, her black eyes peering through her mussed black hair and brightly reflecting the light from the windows.

"You…bitch…" he said, throatily.

He switched his flattening eyes toward Yakima, moved his mouth to say something more, but couldn't manage it. He fell face down on the carpeted floor and lay quivering for a few seconds before falling still.

Yakima stared down at him, his lower jaw hanging. He still had his gun out and unconsciously aimed at the now-dead man on the floor.

He looked at Julia at the same time she looked at him. One...two...three seconds passed, and then she said in a hushed wail, "The door!"

Moving clumsily and a little numbly, as though he'd had a couple of strong shots with the revelers below, Yakima turned and closed the door. He turned back to Julia who stood in front of the desk, facing him, staring at him, her eyes still wide but her expression unreadable. Her brows furled a little and then she seemed to be having trouble placing the big half-breed before her.

Finally, her lips moved and she said quietly, intimately, "Yakima..."

He returned his gaze to the dead man lying in a pool of his own blood on the cream rug and nodded slowly. "Yep, yep...certain-sure...it's me, all right." He returned his befuddled gaze to the pretty, ivory-skinned, rich-lipped, black-haired, black-eyed woman clad in a fancy, dark-blue gown and ruffled shirtwaist before him and said, "So... what's new, Julia?"

Again, her lips trembling this time, she said, "Ya-kima..."

Then she hurried to him, opening her arms. She buried her face in his broad chest and wrapped her arms around him.

"Hold me!"

He did. She felt as she had before. Maybe a little

better though she was trembling. She sobbed against his chest and said, "Just please hold me for a minute. That's all I ask."

Gazing down at the dead man on the floor, Yakima held the trembling girl in his arms. No, she wasn't a girl anymore, but a full-grown woman—twenty-five or -six by now. He couldn't be sure. She looked even better than before and that was saying something. It was as though full womanhood had enhanced her previously raw and girlish features. The bosom pressed against him was full and warm, contracting and expanding as she breathed.

When several minutes had passed and she hadn't said anything but had just kept her arms around him, her face buried in his chest, he snaked his right hand down between them and lifted her chin until her face was tilting up toward his. He glanced at the dead man.

"Who is he, Julia? Why was he threatening you?"

She sniffed, blinked, and brushed tears from her eyes. "Wait."

She turned and walked over to a round table flanking her desk. The table had several crystal glass decanters on it, on a tray with four or five crystal goblets. She lifted the glass stopper from one of the bottles and poured a liberal portion of the liquor into two glasses. She brought one to Yakima.

She looked up at him and closed her rich, bee-stung

lips around the edge of the glass as she lifted it and drank two deep swallows. When she saw that he stood holding his glass in his hand, gazing down at her curiously, she nudged the glass up to his mouth.

He took a sip, lowered the glass, and said, "Now, then…"

"He's a very bad man, Yakima," she said forthrightly, narrowing her long, pretty eyes glistening with emotion as well as the fading, high-country light angling through the curtained windows.

"I sorta gathered that. Leastways, he sure had a burr up his behind. Did you put it there?"

"What?" she asked, widening her eyes in astonishment.

"He said somethin' about rigged gambling games."

She rolled her eyes and took another deep drink from her glass, emptying it halfway. "Two or three of my games are rigged. Every madam in Denver rigs their games. It's understood. It's our way of off-setting the losses from corrupt gamblers!"

The way she'd explained it almost made it sound reasonable. Maybe it did sound reasonable. Or was he just all too influenced by her well-filled, low-cut bodice and the way the sleeves of her gown left her shoulders bare. Her neck was fine and long and smooth behind the screen of her thick, shiny, dark hair.

Those lips. With a silent groan, he couldn't help remembering those magical lips…

He shook his head to refocus his attention. He tried to keep his eyes from roaming lower than her chin, and said, "He said somethin' about *playin'* by his rules…"

She hardened her jaws and narrowed her eyes sparking fury. "He was trying to blackmail me! In return for not turning me in to the authorities, he wanted money. But that's not all he wanted, Yakima." She rammed her thumb between the high, deep valley between her breasts. "He wanted *me!* Whenever he wanted!"

"That scoundrel!" Yakima placed his hands comfortingly on Julia's slender shoulders and cast his own angry gaze now at the rat on the bloody rug. "In that case, he got what he deserved."

"That's how I saw it!" She closed her hand around her neck, flushing. "I thought he was going to strangle me!"

"You're all right, now, darlin'."

"So I killed him!"

"Yeah, yeah—you sure did." Yakima returned his questioning gaze to the pretty madam before him. "How you going to play it? Best get the authorities and explain the whole thing, I reckon. He was trying to strangle you, sure enough."

Julia shook her head. "I don't think that will work."

"Why not?"

"He's a very powerful man."

"How so?"

"Turn him over."

Yakima walked over, leaned down, and rolled the man onto his back.

"Now slide his left coat lapel back."

Yakima did that, as well. He sucked a sharp breath through gritted teeth when the moon-and-star badge of a deputy U.S. marshal, pinned to the man's paisley vest, winked in the near window light.

Chapter 6

"That's not good," Yakima said, rubbing his jaw. "That's not good at all."

"Now you see why I can't go to the authorities?"

Yakima raked his gaze from the deputy U.S. marshal's badge on the dead man's chest to Julia, scowling as he pondered the troubling situation he'd stumbled into.

She said, "He was as crooked as a dog's hind leg!" Julia drew her right foot back then thrust it forward with a shrill cry of deep-seated anger and buried the toe of her high-heeled, leather, side-button shoe, the same blue of her dress, into the man's side.

The man lolled from side to side and shook his head a little, his head and body a little out of sync with each other. The dead lawman stared up at her and her reluctant cohort through half-open eyes. His neck and chest were covered in blood, as was the rug beneath him.

"I don't doubt it a bit," Yakima said. He knew a little about deputy U.S. marshals. He wouldn't say they were all bad, but the ones he'd tangled with had deserved every ounce of the lead he'd drilled them with. He'd been avoiding such men. Now, here he was in a room with a dead one.

This is what he got, he told himself, for cavorting with fallen women!

Julia turned to Yakima, placed her hands on his chest, and gazed up at him with wide-eyed beseeching. "Will you help me?"

Yakima winced. "Don't you have a bouncer...maybe a swamper...or an odd-job man...?"

"None who I trust half as much as I trust you, Yakima." Julia winked at him. Crossing those dark, almond-shaped eyes a little, she smiled alluringly, pressing her fingers more deeply into his pectoral muscles. "I think it's best if we keep this between us—don't you think?" She rose up onto her toes, drew her head up close to Yakima's, stuck her tongue in his left ear, swirled it, then pressed her lips to his.

She kissed him passionately.

Feeling his blood surge and his loins warm and the warm wetness of her tongue lingering in his ear, Yakima wrapped his arms around her and returned the kiss with an equally passionate one of his own.

She drew her head back but keeping her lips very close to his, so close that they moved a little against his own, she tucked his long hair back behind each of his ears and said, "I will make it up to you, Yakima." She smiled. "You know I will." She smiled a little broader until he could see the ends of her fine, white teeth. "As only I can."

She lowered one of her hands between them.

Yakima grunted and more blood surged.

Oh, god—yeah, how well he remembered how only she could do quite a few things to him.

She smiled, showing all her teeth now. She knew she had him.

God blast his carnal cravings, anyways, but, yeah, of course, she had him.

He stepped back and shook his head as though to clear it. "All right," he said, "first things first. Does anyone else know he's here?"

"Probably. I'm sure he came in the front door, so I'm sure some of the girls saw him, but they were getting busy with their clients by then, so they probably won't think anything of him not leaving."

"Even when they find out he's dead?"

Julia winced and turned to a window, crossing her arms and pondering.

Suddenly, she wheeled back to Yakima, her eyes wide. When for nearly a minute she didn't say anything but only stared at Yakima with one hand fingering the black, silk, diamond-studded choker at her neck, Yakima gave a rueful chuff and said, "What is it? What's on your mind, Julia?"

"You won't judge me too harshly?"

"I haven't so far, have I?"

"We need to make him disappear."

"Disappear?"

"No one must find him."

"How are we gonna do that? It's a big city. Not too many places to dispose of a body without anyone—"

"The hog pens down near Union Station."

Yakima glowered back at her in disbelief.

She quirked a wry smile. "They will leave no sign of him. They'll devour every..." She turned her angry eyes to the dead man again and, curling her upper lip, said, "scrap of that animal!"

Still glowering, Yakima said, "How in the hell are we gonna get this deputy marshal's dead carcass down to Union Station without being seen?"

Again, she stepped up close to him. Close enough to press her firm yet supple bosoms against his belly once more and wrap her arms around his neck. "Not *we*. It will have to be you. I'll be expected downstairs, you see, with my clients." She kissed him again, quickly, as though to remind him of the softness of her lips. Quietly, keeping her lips very close to his, she continued with: "You will have to wait until good dark and then haul him down to the stock pens..."

"Haul him in *what?*"

"There's a buckboard in the shed behind the house. Simply wrap him in the rug, carry him downstairs—I'll make sure all the girls are downstairs and no one's in the kitchen, so no one will see you—and throw him in the wagon. Drive the wagon down to the..."

"Stock pens and throw the dead lawman to the pigs," Yakima finished for her, his voice pitched with a low, dark, quiet exasperation.

He'd never had much luck in Denver. Aside from Julia, that was. But now he was starting to wish he'd avoided the city...and her...all together and tried his luck farther north in Cheyenne. There must be a doxie or two with Julia's talents in Cheyenne. Or one who came close, anyway.

As though reading his mind, she kissed him again, pressing her bosoms even more firmly against his chest. She pulled her head away from his, giving his lower lip a sensually painful little bite as she did, and crossed those alluring eyes at him again.

Nah, nah, probably not, he silently amended his speculation.

He was doomed.

***

Being hunted by federal marshals throughout the West, Yakima felt a little uncomfortable being holed up, waiting for dark, with a dead deputy U.S. marshal rolled up in the rug he'd died on.

No, he felt very uncomfortable.

But that's what Yakima did, moving around Julia's tony suite, feeling like a lion locked up in a caged wagon, albeit a gilded cage. He remained holed up with the dead man, waiting for total darkness outside and for the city to settle down a little after its customary nightly revelry.

In the meantime, Julia was downstairs entertaining her clients and performing her duties as a madam as well as overseeing the bar and the gambling layout. She was a busy woman these days, Julia was. Despite the current trouble he'd leaped into fully clothed, Yakima was happy for her.

How she'd been able to move up so quickly and acquire her own place, he didn't know. He hadn't had time to ask. He didn't want to know.

As to the subject of her rigged gambling—well, that was another thing he really didn't care to know about.

Who was he to judge?

As he sat in her desk chair, swiveling this way and that, playing with things on her desk, smoking cigarettes, and sipping whiskey, he could hear her down in the hurdy-gurdy house's main drinking hall, charming the clientele. Occasionally, she sent a bawdy laugh hurling into the floor beneath Yakima's moccasins. A few times, he heard her hurrying to the scene of an argument breaking out between two or three jakes and quieting them down with Julia's firm but gentle and amused aplomb, buying drinks for the house.

A whoop went up and the gent playing the piano ripped into "Little Brown Jug"!

They were having fun down there. Yakima would like to have been part of it. But even if he didn't have a dead man to dispose of, he could not have been. His kind was not welcome in a place like this. Even if there were no actual signs up forbidding access to Indians or half-breeds or Mexicans or Negros or Chinamen, the virtual signs were everywhere in a place like this.

Of course, that only made him want to challenge said prejudices and go down there and stomp with his half-breed tail up. But no, no, no.

He had a dead man to dispose of.

Then he'd return to Julia's boudoir and be amply rewarded.

That made him smile and remember earlier times with Julia fondly. She was looking even better than before. She'd likely treat him even better than she had before, after he'd performed his chore for her. Of course, he realized she was using him, but pretty women had used him before. He could suck down his pride and do what needed to be done.

After all, what choice did he have? Someone had to dispose of the body. His having stumbled into Julia's suite just when she'd killed the man had made him an accomplice to the man's murder. He, already a wanted man—for the killings of other lawmen, no less! Now the evidence had to be disposed of. He was the only one to do it.

Served him right for coming into town, anyway. Damn fool thing to do. His loins would be the death of him one day.

He hadn't realized he'd fallen asleep, kicked back in Julia's chair, his ankles crossed on her desk, until a light knock on the door woke him.

Yakima strode to the door, unlocked and opened it. Julia stood before him, looking radiant and flushed from the enervation he'd only been privy to via the sounds through the floor. Her dark eyes sparkled in the candlelit hall. The smell of tobacco smoke and liquor mixed with her perfume.

"It's time," she said, smiling up at Yakima. "The cook has left and all the girls and their jakes are downstairs for a party. It's the birthday of one our regular customers." She broadened her smile. "The mayor of Denver's brother in law. Julia raised a hand to her mouth to add covertly, "The mayor's even here!"

She leaned forward, lowered her head and tittered a laugh. Apparently remembering that the situation up here was far graver than the one down below, she snapped an anxious, sympathetic look up at Yakima standing over her. "Oh, forgive me, Yakima! You've been hidden away up here with"—she glanced around him at the body rolled up in the carpet, and hardened her jaws as well as her eyes—"*him!*"

She placed a hand on the half-breed's forearm, gave it an affectionate squeeze. "Thank you, Yakima. You're an absolute darling. I'll make it up to you, I promise. At midnight, I always kiss a few cheeks and say my good-nights and head up here to my rooms." She flounced on her hips and batted her eyelashes. "By the time you return, it should be the witching hour. I'll leave the key in the door for you!"

She winked bewitchingly, rose onto her toes, planted a quick kiss on his lips, then strode off down the hall. When she gained the top of the stairs, she hiked her silk and satin gown up above her ankles and dropped down out of sight. Below, several men clapped and howled and one whistled at the madam's return.

Yakima cursed and stepped back into the crypt, which was how he'd come to see Julia's fancy digs complete with dead deputy U.S. marshal rolled up in the carpet. He walked over crouched, and back-and-bellied the man and the rug up onto his shoulder. The rug was about eight feet long, so it adequately concealed the body if he happened to come upon someone in the hall.

He was glad that he did not.

Nor in the narrow rear hall.

Nor in the kitchen.

He had quite a time negotiating his way through the kitchen with the eight-foot burial shroud and two tight corners to work his way around. Once he'd finally gained the outside with its thick, concealing darkness and the chill night, high-country air of late summer, he heaved a sigh of massive relief.

The four hours he'd spent upstairs in Julia's suite might have been the longest four hours of his life. What a contrast to the bedroom high-jinx he'd expected!

He adjusted the blanket-wrapped dead man on his shoulder, grunting beneath the strain, and started walking straight out away from the parlor house. The shed was a pale blur in the darkness ahead maybe a hundred feet. A privy sat before it, just ahead and to Yakima's right. He took another step and stopped suddenly when from somewhere nearby a man laughed. Another muttered something that Yakima couldn't make out.

His heart lurched as he froze, dropped to a knee and,

balancing the blanket-wrapped dead man on his shoulder, turned his head to follow the voices to their source.

He saw two silhouetted figures standing off the two-hole privy's right front corner. By the dribbling sounds he could hear in the now-quiet night, two men were evacuating their bladders over there. Judging by the sounds coming from behind the privy door, at least one man, possibly two, were doing business inside the latrine itself.

The smell of tobacco smoke emanated from that direction, as well.

One of the men standing outside, his back to Yakima, said, "She came far in a short amount of time, Miss Julia did—I'll give her that. A year ago she was still workin' the line at Skeeter Wallace's club. Now she's got her own fancy hurdy-gurdy house with some of the sweetest whores in Denver!"

A man inside the privy grunted a laugh and said, "She's got a knack for convincing powerful men to do powerful things for her. And I mean a *knack!*" He laughed again.

"Whatever works," said the second standing man.

Yeah, whatever works, Yakima wryly thought.

He heaved himself back to both feet, trying not grunt against the strain of the dead man and rug on his shoulder. He hurried forward, hoping like hell neither of the two standing men heard him and turned to see him, and that neither man in the privy—if there were two—spied his moving shadow through the cracks between the privy's vertical, white-painted planks.

He heard more voices just as he reached the shed's front door—more men likely sauntering out of the brothel to tend nature. They were talking and laughing. He could hear the piano, as well.

Yakima set the body and the rug down to open the shed door. As he did, he glanced over his right shoulder. The men milling around the privies were murky shadows. They were talking and laughing, joking among themselves.

Quickly, Yakima slid the shed door open then crouched to drag the rug-wrapped deputy inside and out of sight. He cursed under his breath.

That had been close. He hadn't considered men using the privy. He should have and Julia should have, too but neither he nor she, apparently, had.

No, wait. He knelt to stare out the two-foot gap in the shed door.

He thought he'd heard Julia's voice. He held his breath and pricked his ears, listening.

Sure enough, it was her all right.

"Come on back inside, gentlemen—each and every one of you!" she hailed the men at the privy. "I'm going to buy just one more round and head to bed! Come and get it while supplies last!"

The men yelled raucously, several clapping their hands. In less than a minute, Yakima watched the last shadow drift on back around the saloon to the front. Silence settled over the privy and the shed—silence save for the muffled roar of the crowd inside the brothel and the energetic pattering of the piano.

Quickly, Yakima roped one of the two horses, a blooded sorrel mare, he found contentedly munching hay in the small corral flanking the shed. He hitched the mount to the buckboard wagon that Julia's hired help must have used for supply runs such as stocking the whorehouse larder and such. He'd spied a leather buggy at the back of the shed, as well, likely what she used for fetching important, moneyed clients from Union Station, perhaps?

My, my, Yakima thought as he shook the reins over the sorrel's back and slowly rolled out of the shed, the wheels crunching gravel and the short, tough brown grass that grew in this area flanking the brothel. The dead lawman lay in the carpet in the box, the shadows of the box concealing the man and the rug from view.

He took the backstreets down toward Union Station.

He drove more slowly when he came to the stock pens reeking of cows and pigs and even chickens penned up in preparation for being loaded onto a train likely headed for Kansas City or Chicago. He stopped the wagon in the heavy shadows cast by a water tower along the tracks and carried the rug-shrouded body over to where he could smell and hear the telltale snorting of hogs.

He moved slowly, crouching, his jaws and his backbone tense, on the alert for the railyard bulls who patrolled the stockyard nightly. If there were any out here, he didn't see any.

When he came to the hog pens, he tossed the dead lawman, rug and all, into the pen. Judging by the snorts that climbed quickly into raucous, ravenous squeals, the hogs didn't have any trouble finding their midnight snack. Yakima high-tailed it in a full run back to the wagon, clambered aboard, released the brake, turned the sorrel around and headed back in the direction from which he'd come.

He tensed, heart quickening, when a man's shrill voice bellowed from a good distance behind him, "What in God's name has those pigs carryin' on about?"

"Hey, up there—a wagon!" a second man shouted.

Yakima slapped the reins over the sorrel's back, urging more speed.

"Hey, you—*stop!*" came a shout from behind.

It was followed by two sharp cracks of a pistol and then one more.

One of the bullets plowed into the front panel of the wagon box just inches below where Yakima sat on the seat. He ducked as he swerved around the corner of a cow pen and raced hell-bent back east and in the direction of Denver proper.

He kept to the back streets until he was safely back in the shed after having carefully scouted the area around the privy and finding it vacant. The din inside the saloon had dwindled considerably. Maybe the festivities were over. He'd return to Julia's boudoir and collect his bounty.

He returned the sorrel to the corral then left the shed.

Wanting to get the lay of the land inside, he walked around to the front of the brothel and peered through a side window.

Maybe only a quarter of the previous crowd remained in the main drinking hall. So did Julia. She was dancing a slow waltz with a tall, blond-haired man in a soldier's uniform, a lieutenant's bars on his shoulders. A stocky but refined-looking man in a red satin vest over a crisp white shirt and boasting a handlebar mustache stood before them, playing a violin.

A dozen or so remaining jakes—all dressed to the nines, their mustaches and beards professionally trimmed, pomade in their hair—stood in a circle around the dancers, watching dreamily, drinks and cigarettes or cigars in their hands.

No, the night was not yet over.

But Yakima's was.

He smiled at the serenely smiling Julia being waltzed

by the handsome soldier. He chuckled, shook his head.

She'd moved on.

It was time for him to do the same thing.

He stepped away from the window and stuck to the backstreet shadows as he strolled back to the livery barn. He found his way into the stall Wolf shared with Paul's mule, Ol' Angus. The horse whickered an affectionate greeting. Yakima kissed the horse's snout and tusseled its ears, patted its withers.

"Just you an' me, old boy. That's the best way."

He shucked out of his hat and boots, kicked up a pile of hay in a corner of the stall, and threw himself into it like a kid diving into a creek. Instantly, he was out like a blown lamp.

"Hey, Yakima," Sven Norgaard said the next morning, as Yakima left the stall tucking his shirt into his pants. "How come you ain't over to Julia's?"

Yakima spat to one side and dug his makings out of his shirt pocket. "Her rates got too damn high, Sven. Just too damn high."

Chapter 7

Norgaard was about to respond when he stopped suddenly and turned his head to one side, listening. Yakima stopped about ten feet from the tall blond liveryman, who stood between the livery barn's open double doors, in a buttery wash of clear morning sunshine. Yakima, too, had heard the clomp of hooves on the street cobbles as well as the English-accented voices.

"...check here and then down the street," said one of the approaching riders, his voice sounding oddly nasal. "My gut tells me he's still in town. Riding with the Bengal Lancers taught me to always listen to my gut, by bloody God! If he's here, with all the coppers we have lookin' for him, too, we'll root him out, by bloody Christ!"

Norgaard jerked his anxious, wide-eyed gaze to Yakima.

Yakima lurched around to regard his horse and the

mule. They were in the last stall on the left side of the barn alley, not visible from outside, most likely. But if the earl and his men decided to investigate the barn, they'd see them, all right. Yakima had no time to lead them out the back. The head of one of the approaching horses was already entering his field of vision.

He glanced again at Norgaard. He didn't say anything. Nothing needed to be said. He and Sven were old friends. He knew what to do.

Quickly, Yakima opened the stall door, stepped inside, latched the door, and dropped to a knee to stare through a crack between the door and the stall partition.

As he did, Norgaard swung around to face the approaching riders, fashioning a friendly smile on his broad, blue-eyed, Scandinavian face. "Well, good-mornin' there, gentlemen. And what a fine Rocky Mountain morning it is too, is it not?"

The man with the nasal voice, likely the earl, only grumbled something that Yakima couldn't make out. Then, peering through the crack, he saw the earl and three other men, all as outlandishly attired as the red-headed, red-mustached Earl of Cork, ride up to the front of the barn. Their fine, sleek mounts with silver tack fittings glistened in the Colorado sunshine.

So did the large bandage covering the Earl of Cork's badly swollen and darkened nose. The man eyes were swollen and dark, as well. They were so swollen that the small, round, steel-rimmed spectacles he wore had drifted down low on his broken nose.

He shoved them up with a gloved thumb and, looking none too pleased about his no-doubt aching condition and scowling sneeringly down at Norgaard, said, "Shut up, you toadish lout. I don't care about the damned morning. We're lookin' for a big half-breed who rode into town on a black horse and was leading a mule yesterday in the late afternoon. We were told that someone saw him riding near here. Have you seen him?"

"Big half-breed, you say," Norgaard said, lifting his chin and scratching it, as though pondering deeply on the query. "Big half-breed...hmmm... Say, that nose looks sore!"

"Have you seen him? The local constabulary seem to think he might be Yakima Henry. A wanted man. Wanted for murder, in fact. Of federal marshals."

"Yakima Henry...Yakima Henry..." Sven said, turning his head to one side so that Yakima could see him still rubbing his chin and stretching his lips back from his teeth as though in deep reflection. "Hmmm," he said finally. "You know, the name does sound familiar, but I ain't seen hide nor hair of *any* big half-breed. At least, not in the past day or two."

"Are you sure?" the earl asked skeptically.

"Yep, yep—I'm certain-sure. I can understand your anger, though, if it was him that done that to your—"

"Maybe we'll just take a look inside," the earl said, swinging down from his saddle and sliding a pretty, long-barreled hogleg from one of the two holsters buckled outside of his brightly beaded buckskin coat. He showed his teeth through a sneer at the liveryman. "You wouldn't mind, would you, Mr. Nordegaard. I'm assuming you're Nordegaard…"

"Well, now, I—" Nordegaard stopped when the two other outlandishly attired English popinjays swung down from their saddles and drew their own pistols, glowering at the big blond liveryman. "I, uh…I reckon not. Sure, sure," he said, glancing toward Yakima, worry showing in the rigid set of his cheeks and in his eyes. "I…reckon…"

Yakima grabbed his Henry repeater from off the top of his gear and trail possibles piled nearby. Staying low, he very slowly and quietly levered a round into the Yellowboy's action and held the rifle straight up and down before him. He stared through the crack as the four men entered the barn, aiming their pistols out in front of them. They came in single file, the earl in the lead.

The broken-nosed dandy moved slowly down the barn's alley, swinging his head from right to left, peering into the stalls around him. The bandage glowed white in the barn's dark shadows.

The earl strode slowly forward, the other three flanking him, backing him, pistols gripped tightly in their gloved hands. William Anthony Boyle drew to within twenty feet of where Yakima knelt, peering through the crack in the stall partition, tightening his index finger around the Yellowboy's trigger, heart tattooing a warning rhythm against his breastbone.

As the earl took another step forward, Yakima prepared to raise the Winchester. If he had to, he'd kill the man. He had a feeling he'd very likely have to. He'd been a fool to do what he'd done out in the street the day before and drawn attention to himself when he already had several bounties on his head and had wanted to slip in and out of town unnoticed.

But breaking the mouthy earl's nose was just his way. Sometimes he was a damn slave to those ways. Those ways would very likely get him killed, probably sooner rather than later. But he'd be damned if this British popinjay was going to be the one to punch his ticket.

He'd drill a round right through the center of the man's freckled forehead, beneath the broad brim of his silly cream, silk-banded sombrero and then he'd taken the other three down—*bang, bang, bang, bang!*

Then hightail it for the tall and uncut...

The earl took one more step forward, and then as he swung his eyes from left to right, his gaze held on Wolf and the mule peering out over the stall partition.

Now's the time, Yakima thought.

He started to jerk up the Yellowboy.

He stopped when an English-accented voice outside the barn yelled, "Bryce, tell Willie that Giffie and Carlisle saw a drunk half-breed fitting our man's description stumbling out of an alley near the Larimer! They've got him on the run. We're headed that way!"

The earl had stopped and peered behind him, listening.

"You hear that?" asked one of the men behind him.

The earl turned his head back forward, incredulously regarding Wolf and the mule staring back at him. He stretched his lips angrily back from his teeth then spun sharply and ran back toward the doors. "I heard! Let's go, gentlemen!"

As he ran past Nordegaard, he glared at the man and barked, "You haven't seen him, eh? Then why are his horse and mule in your barn? *Liar!*" he added throatily with menace.

He swung up into the saddle, as did his three compatriots. They reined their horses around and booted them back in the direction from which they'd come, shod hooves clacking on the cobbles.

Nordegaard turned back toward Yakima, who rose, depressing the Winchester's hammer. Nordegaard glared at him, hard-jawed, indignant. "You're trouble, you know that?" He pointed at the big half-breed as though there might be some question whom he was addressing. "Always have been, for as long as I've known you. And you always will be!"

"I 'spect." Yakima leaned his rifle down then crouched to pick up his saddle blanket and threw the blanket over Wolf's back. "I'll just be on my way now, Sven. Sorry I can't linger over coffee."

"Hell, I'll help you!" the liveryman said, striding quickly toward the stable. "I can't get you out of here fast enough. Oh, and by the way, you owe me six dollars for the grub and another dollar for the trouble."

Yakima paused in his work to toss the man a ten-dollar gold eagle. "Keep the change. Keep the mule, too. It's a good mule, so treat him right. He belonged to a good friend of mine."

Nordekker looked stunned as he glanced from Yakima to Ol' Angus and back again. "What?"

"He'll only slow me down. I gotta make some fast tracks." Yakima glanced at the mule staring at him, twitching each ear in turn. "Sorry, fella. Sven will find a good home for you, though—won't you, Sven?"

Nordekker walked around the mule, inspecting the big beast. "Yeah, hell…he's in good shape. Maybe a little extra tallow on him, but he'll go for a fair price, I reckon." He glanced at Yakima. "What happened to your friend?"

"He's dead."

Nordekker drew his mouth corners down and gave a grim nod.

He watched silently as Yakima led Wolf out of the stall and down the barn alley to the open front doors, moving quickly, his back taut, ears pricked for the sound of approaching horses.

Nordekker followed him, jostling the eagle in his hand. He said, "Yakima, next time you're in Denver—"

"Don't worry, this is my last visit." Yakima stopped Wolf just outside the barn and swung up into the leather. "I should have avoided this dung hill in the first place. But what did I do? First thing I did when I entered town, I busted that prissy fool's nose for him."

"An' you didn't even get no satisfaction from Miss Julia?"

"Hell, no. Like I said, her prices are too damn high!"

Nordekker nodded. "That's the word goin' around."

"Thanks, Sven." Yakima pinched his hat brim at the man and neck-reined Wolf out into the street. "Sorry for the trouble."

"Yakima?"

The half-breed stopped and looked back at the liveryman. Nordekker gave him a reluctant half-smile. "I meant to say next time you're in Denver...*when* you return and you *will* return sooner or later because it's never been like you to avoid trouble...you got a place to hole up right here."

He shrugged a broad shoulder.

Yakima returned the man's smile, pinched his hat brim to him.

He booted Wolf on down the street, in the opposite direction from that in which the earl and the earl's men had ridden. They'd likely be back this way soon.

Chapter 8

Two nights later, somewhere in the sagebrush buttes northeast of Cheyenne, Yakima sat on the shoulder of a bluff staring northward. Dakota Territory spread out dark and forbidding before him under a night sky that resembled a vast, black velvet blanket sprinkled with glittering sequins lit from within.

His fire lay behind him, lower on the bluff's far side and shielded from view by one large boulder and several stunt cottonwoods. The night was so still and quiet he could hear it crackling faintly. He occasionally caught a whiff of the smoke it sent out. He kept it only large enough to keep his coffee pot warm.

He sat with his knees raised, arms wrapped around them, his half-empty coffee cup in one hand. His low-crowned, flat-brimmed black hat sat on the ground to his left.

He glowered off into the darkness as loneliness assailed him. It was like a rot in his belly. He wasn't used to it and he now knew why he'd ridden into Denver despite the bounties on his head. At least in Denver the wolves of loneliness had been held at bay. True, he'd gotten himself in a whole mess of trouble and had, of all things, tossed a dead lawman to the hogs to help save a young woman from ruin. But at least he hadn't felt lonely doing it!

Out here, the loneliness wolves were on the prowl, circling, growling, snarling. He could almost see their eyes glowing red as hot coals in the starlight, hear the soft padding of their sneaky feet.

They'd found him before, but they'd usually disappeared after a few days. What had brought them now was Paul's death. Yakima had genuinely enjoyed the man's company and had taken comfort in their unusual companionship. It had been a welcome relief from his solitary existence. After his German prospector father and his full-blooded Cheyenne mother had passed when he'd still been a young man and before he'd woken in that Arizona jail with Paul Cahill, there'd been only two other people in his life.

Ralph and Faith.

As with Paul, he'd been close friends with Ralph.

Of course, his relationship with Faith had been a whole other thing. He'd loved her. Only after she'd entered his life, in fact, had he realized what love really was. It was becoming part of someone else. It was someone else becoming part of you. In fact, that someone else was sometimes more you than you yourself were.

When Faith had died in his arms, he'd spent months, years even, feeling as though part of his soul had been ripped out of him. He still felt that way. Maybe he always would. Once part of your soul is gone, there's no getting it back. Not ever. Not even if he happened to fall in love again, which he didn't think would happen.

There'd only been one love in his life and that had been Faith.

Now, defying his better judgement and indulging his darkest thoughts, he realized that the reason he felt so ravaged now was not only because Paul was gone but because his death reminded him of Faith's death. It reminded him, too, that there would never be another Faith. Maybe a woman. He hoped a woman sometime. But never Faith.

He was alone.

As if to confirm that assessment, a long, forlorn wolf's howl rose from somewhere in the dark country to the northeast of him. That feeling of aching rot in his belly intensified. He was glad for the distraction of seeing another fire in that direction. Not a small one like his, but a fairly large one, judging by the size of its glow. It appeared to be in the low country maybe a mile or a mile and a half from his position, in a broad bowl between buttes.

He frowned, curious.

He hadn't seen the blaze until now though he'd scouted the country carefully several times after sundown, always on the lookout for signs of other travelers—travelers who might have shadowed him out from Denver.

Bounty hunters, say.

He studied the fire over the rim of his coffee cup.

Who was over there? Why had they built their fire that large? True, it was a cool October night, but you'd have to be mighty cold, and foolish, to build a fire that size. It was the mark of someone comfortable enough in the country to not feel the danger such a fire could attract, which might mean drovers from a nearby ranch. Possibly some pilgrim who didn't know better, or someone wanting to attract attention to themselves.

Possibly someone wanting to attract *Yakima's* attention and thus draw him into the trap of checking it out. That would likely mean either lawmen or bounty hunters. Unless the Earl of Cork was still mad enough to have followed him this far from Denver. That was doubtful.

Which left bounty hunters or lawmen.

He thought about it then shook his head, nixing the idea. Bounty hunters or lawmen wouldn't be foolish enough to think he'd be foolish enough to walk into such an obvious trap.

Who, then?

Impossible to know. It probably didn't have anything to do with him, anyway. He was just overcautious, over-thinking it. On the other hand, being who and what he was, it paid to be cautious and to overthink some things.

He finished his coffee, donned his hat, rose and re-turned to his fire to refill his cup. Once his cup was again filled with the coal black brew that steamed in the chilly night, he kicked dirt on the fire. No point taking unnec-essary chances. When he turned in for the night, he'd wear his three-point capote beneath his blankets. That was all he needed. He'd do nothing more, he promised himself, to attract attention to himself.

He'd avoid towns and silly scuffles. He'd avoid women most of all.

He'd made a promise to Paul to get that letter and the money belt to his son and that's what he aimed to do.

What would he do after that?

He returned to his previous place—a comfortable little hollow padded with grass on the bluff's shoulder and sat down to ponder out the question. He lay on one side, legs crossed at the ankles, resting on one elbow. He held the cup on the ground before him. As he absently, with little remaining interest, kept his eye on the distant fire, he considered his options for the winter.

He wouldn't return to Colorado. Too hot for him there.

Wyoming, maybe, though the winters there could be colder than a grave-digger's ass. Not like Dakota, though. No place barring Canada was as cold as Dakota. He knew that from experience. Especially northern Dakota though the entire vast territory was no picnic after, say, September.

Here, it was already October. The temperature dropped to below freezing at night.

"Stop complainin'," he told himself. "You made a promise. You're going fulfill it and then get the hell down south—somewhere, anywhere—as fast as ol' Wolf can carry your raggedy half-breed ass!"

Where would he go?

Pondering the question only stirred up the wolves again. In fact, he fell asleep right there, before he'd even finished his coffee, listening to the yammering of distant wolves though their mournful yowls were oddly comforting, as though the lamentations of kindred spirits.

"Good-night, Yakima."

"Good-night, Paul."

***

As usual, he was up at dawn's first blush.

He built up his fire to make coffee. He sat on the bluff's

eastern slope, watching the throbbing liquid ochre orb of the sun climb out of the far eastern plain, thrusting bayonets of scarlet and saffron across the sky banded with high, thin clouds. He sipped his coffee, felt the chill breeze, which was building with the sun's rise, push against him, refreshing him, making him feel better.

So, he was alone. He was a loner at heart.

And he had a job to do. All he need think about was fulfilling his promise to Paul. Tomorrow, there'd be another sunrise like this one for him to enjoy. The next day and the next day and forever after until he, like Paul… and Faith…and Ralph…was planted on some lonely windswept bluff with a view of the setting and rising sun.

He ate some jerky, drank his coffee, saddled Wolf and broke camp.

He'd no sooner slid his Yellowboy into its scabbard and stepped into the saddle than a scream cut through the quiet morning air. He jerked his head to stare off toward the north, his pulse quickening. It had been a girl's scream. It came again, again, and again.

It was followed by a man's bellowing wail.

The sounds were originating from the same low area in which Yakima had spied the large fire the previous night. Now he could see the murky shapes of several figures moving just beyond a brush-lined creek that bisected the low area between bluffs, running from east to west, from his right to his left.

A man's shout came again, followed by another terrified scream from the girl. The girl's scream hadn't died before Yakima ground his heels into Wolf's flanks and the horse lunged forward into an instant, ground-churning gallop. The stallion dropped quickly down the side of the bluff and stretched its stride across the flat toward the creek. Yakima could no longer see the figures, for he was too low now and the brush lining the creek was between him and them.

The girl was obviously in trouble, though.

Or were there more than one?

He heard now the cries of a what sounded like a younger child. The closer he drew to the creek, within fifty yards and closing quickly, he could more clearly hear the young girl's cries of, "Annie! Annie! Don't hurt my sister!"

The older girl screamed, "*No!* Get your hands off me!"

A man yelped.

Another man laughed.

Yakima reined Wolf to a skidding halt, shucked the Yellowboy from its scabbard, and leaped from the saddle. He bulled through the brush lining the creek, ran across the creek which was only a few inches deep, then bounded through the brush on the opposite bank.

Just beyond the brush, he stopped.

A man stood just ahead and to his left. He was holding a little girl whose brown-haired head came up to the buckle of his cartridge belt. Dressed in a ragged trail attire, including leather chaps and badly weathered Stetson, he stared toward where another man, similarly attired, just then cracked the back of his right hand across the right cheek of an older girl, a blond in a plain blouse, a gray wool skirt and black ankle boots.

The girl screamed and flew backward, her long hair flying about her shoulders.

"That's what you get for kickin' me you little polecat! Now you'd better be a little nicer to me or—"

The man stopped and wheeled just as Yakima, striding quickly up to the man holding the little girl, smashed his Winchester's barrel across the back of that man's head.

"Hey!" bellowed the man who'd been abusing the girl.

He was tall and beefy and sunburned. He wore no hat though a funnel-brimmed cream Stetson lay on the ground nearby. His face was broad and mustached and his eyes were sharp with rage. He stretched his lips back from tobacco-grimed teeth and started to reach for the Schofield revolver holstered on his right thigh but had only started to pull the smoke wagon when the Yellowboy bucked twice in Yakima's hands.

The first bullet took the would-be rapist high in the middle of his chest.

A second later, the second bullet drilled into his chest

four inches below the first one.

Both bullets sent him dancing backwards, pinwheeling and dropping. He rolled onto his back, grinding his shoulders and heels into the ground, arching his back. He gave a shrill final cry and collapsed on his back. He turned his head toward Yakima and his amber eyes glazed in death.

Lying on the ground to the right of her dead attacker, the blond girl pointed and yelled, "Look out!"

Yakima wheeled. The man he'd brained lay on the ground off Yakima's left flank. Blood dribbled from both nostrils. He gritted his teeth as he raised the Colt .44 in his right hand, sliding the barrel toward Yakima.

The Winchester crashed twice more.

The man triggered the Colt wild just before he dropped it and fell back against the ground, shivering as he died.

Chapter 9

The two girls looked around, eyes wide and round with disbelief.

They looked at each dead man in turn, shifting their frightened gazes to Yakima standing with the smoking Winchester still raised to his shoulder. Slowly, he lowered the rifle to his side and turned to the older girl, the blond, who lay where she'd fallen, resting on one elbow.

Her torn blouse hung off one pale shoulder. Dirt and dead leaves clung to her skirt. Her lower lip was split and a red welt had risen on her left cheek, where the larger of the two dead men had walloped her.

Yakima said, "Are you all—"

He stopped when the blond looked at the younger girl sitting with her legs stretched out in front of her, beneath her wool skirt, pantaloon showing between her skirt and ankle boots. Large tears rolled down her cheeks from terror-bright eyes.

"Beth!" the blond cried, heaving herself to her feet and running over to the little one. She dropped to her knees before the girl who, judging by their similarities in appearance, was her sister.

She swept the child up in her arms. "Oh, Beth!"

Beth hadn't made a sound up to then but now she bawled against her sister's shoulder, wrapping her arms and legs tightly around her, as though she never wanted to let her go again.

Yakima decided to give the two some privacy.

He looked around, wanting to be sure there were no other cutthroats in the area. When he spied just two horses tied to a couple of cottonwoods roughly fifty yards west along the stream, he dragged each dead man away by his ankles, depositing them together in a shallow wash east of the girl's camp. As he did, he spied the still-smoldering remains of a fire around which trail gear was piled neatly, just beyond where the two girls knelt together, the older one comforting the younger one, talking to her softly and combing her short brown hair gently with her fingers.

The fire he'd spied last night from the bluff had obviously been the girls' fire.

Finished dragging the dead men off where the girls wouldn't see them to be reminded of the horror they'd endured, Yakima looked around more thoroughly. There was no sign of the girls having any stock—no horses or mules. No wagon, either.

No sign, in fact, of their being in the company of anyone else. No mother or father. The gear strewn around the fire was damned spare—only a few grub sacks and blankets and one ragged doll with red hair made from dyed cornhusks and clad in blue denim overalls. A half-eaten ham sandwich lay on a blanket beside an overturned tin cup.

Yakima switched his curious gaze to the girls. They sat together now, the older one holding the hand of the younger one, regarding him silently, warily.

"You two alone out here?" he asked.

The pair looked at each other. They turned back to Yakima, and the blond one shook her head. "Pa's off huntin' is all." She glanced around. "Should be back anytime."

"Where's his gear?"

The blond glanced at the grub sacks and blankets strewn around the smoldering gray ashes of last night's fire then returned her gaze to the half-breed. "He took it with him."

"I see."

"Thanks for your help, mister." The blond took the younger girl's hand and patted it reassuringly. "We'll be all right now. Like I said, Pa'll be back soon. Anytime now, most likely."

"I see," Yakima said.

The young girl studied him suspiciously. "Are you an Injun?" she asked, beetling her thin brown eyebrows.

The blond, whom Yakima judged to be in her early teens and was pretty with lilac eyes, her naturally fair cheeks lightly tanned, frowned at the younger girl but didn't say anything. Instead, she switched her gaze back to Yakima, as if awaiting his response.

"Half," Yakima said.

"That's all right," the blond said quickly. "W-we don't mind. I mean..." she let her voice trail off, obviously having trouble finding the right thing to say.

"You two are alone out here," Yakima said.

"Uh-uh," the younger girl said, gazing up at the blond, who kept her pretty but frightened lilac gaze on Yakima.

"Where are you headed? You an' your pa..."

"We're just out huntin'," said the younger one, glancing up at the older one again. "Ain't that right, Annie?"

"That's right," Annie said, quickly, nodding. "He should be back anytime, though. Thanks for..." She glanced over toward where Yakima had dragged off the attackers. "You know..." she said and lifted her right cheek in a slight wince, as though recalling the savage attack on her and her sister.

"He must have ridden far enough off that he didn't hear the shooting," Yakima said, looking off into the distance.

"Or he'd have been back by now."

"Probably got on the trail of something," Annie said.

"Followed it a long way. Odd for a fellow to leave his two daughters all alone out here, though."

"Like I said," the blond said, a touch of annoyance in her voice. "He probably got on the trail of something, Pa did."

"Yeah," Beth said. "He probably got on the trail of something."

Yakima drew a deep breath and shouldered his rifle. The matter of these girls bothered him. He didn't want it to. He wanted to hop back atop his stallion and continue his journey north, untroubled, but he found himself lingering.

He narrowed an accusatory eye at the pair. "You two are alone out here."

Annie shook her head and started to say something, but Yakima cut her off with, "There are only two sets of tracks around that fire. Girl-sized tracks. No sign of a horse. No tracks, no dung, no feed, nothing. I doubt a grown man would have built up that fire as big as the one I saw last night from my own camp yonder. You know who would build a fire up that big?"

He didn't wait for the girls to respond. "Two frightened kids. Maybe heard the wolves howlin' and got scared enough to build up the fire so big that every cutthroat within twenty miles could have seen it. You're lucky only two did. You're also lucky I saw it…and heard your screams this morning. Now, tell me the truth this time— what are you two doing alone out here? My skin may be a little too red for you, but if I'd wanted to harm either one of you, I would have by now."

They both just stared at him, confused and scared.

When neither one said anything for nearly a full minute, Yakima said, "All right. I'm goin'." He turned away and started walking back toward the brush lining the stream. He stopped, glanced over his shoulder at the frightened pair once more and said, "Tomorrow night, do both yourselves a favor and keep your fire small."

Yakima walked back through the brush, crossed the stream, climbed the opposite bank, and grabbed Wolf's reins. He slid his rifle back into its scabbard and swung into the leather.

Brush crackled behind him.

He turned to see Annie step out of the shrubs lining the stream bank. A branch caught a lock of her hair; the morning sunlight caught it, as well and it shone like spun honey. She turned to free the hair from the branch then turned to Yakima. She wore a floppy-brimmed black hat now.

She stopped in front of the brush. "Mister?"

Yakima waited.

"We're alone, Beth an' me."

"Where's your folks."

Annie drew a breath, released it slowly, glanced off, her upper lip trembling slightly. She returned her gaze to Yakima and said, "Ma died last winter. There was an influenza outbreak. Mister Henricks—he's our step-pa—treated us awful, Beth an' me. He came in my room one night. He was drunk. I fought him off, but he tried it again a few days later and I hit him over the head with his own bottle. Knocked him out."

Yakima turned Wolf full around to face the girl straight on. "You ran away?"

She nodded as she looked down at the fingers she was steepling together in front of her. "He'd have beat me once he woke up. He would have beat Beth, too…to punish me. That's how he is."

"Nice man, this Mister Henricks. Why'd your mother marry him?"

"He wasn't so bad before Ma died. Besides, our real Pa was dead and Mister Henricks had money, a small ranch. But after Ma died, he took to drinkin' heavy. So Beth and I stuffed some food into a couple of bags, saddled a horse, and rode away before he woke up."

Yakima glanced around again. "Where's your horse?"

"Got spooked by a lightning storm one night. Jerked his picket pin free and ran off. Probably ran back to the ranch."

Yakima nodded slowly, studying the girl before him. "Where you headed?"

She canted her head toward the northwest. "Hat Creek Station." Hat Creek was a relay station along the Cheyenne-to-Black Hills Stagecoach route.

"What for?"

"I figured me an' Beth would look for work there. I need to build us up a stake so we can ride up north to Cannonball. That's where our grandparents on Ma's side live. They'll take us in—I hope leastways. In the meantime, I've heard that Mister Slater at Hat Creek is always hiring."

Yakima looked at her, frowning. "How old are you two?"

"Beth's eight. I'm fifteen."

"Awfully young to be working at the Hat Creek Station." The station, which doubled as a saloon and brothel, with hog pens, or cribs, out behind the main building, was a notorious owlhoot stop-over, almost as famous as Ma Tatum's Saloon down in the Indian Nations.

Annie glanced down, coloring. "I aim to work in the kitchen. Beth, too. And do clean-up work. Mister Slater is always needing clean-up help. I know because a hired-hand of Mister Henricks's—that's our step-pa—always said when Mister Henricks was too tough on him that he could always find better work and higher pay at the Hat Creek Station, where they're always needin' help. He told me I could do that, too, if it ever got too hard at the ranch with Mister Henricks."

"I see," Yakima said. "Well, you'll be safer there than out here. I tell you what, I'll help you get started on one of the horses those two trail wolves left. Adjust the stirrups an' such. Would that be all right?"

Annie smiled, nodded. "Thank you. That would be right nice of you."

Yakima rode up to her and extended his hand to her. "Hop up."

She placed her slender, pale hand in his big, red-brown one and he lifted her up behind him. She placed her hands on his hip, and then he nudged the horse through the brush, following a game trail.

"You didn't tell us your name," Annie said as he put Wolf across the creek.

"Yakima."

"Is that an Indian name?"

"I reckon it is."

"You got a last name?"

"Henry. Yakima Henry."

"Hmm."

"Yep."

Yakima booted Wolf up the opposite bank and over to where Beth stood near where she'd been standing before, looking worried. She looked skeptically up at her sister riding behind the big, long-haired red man.

Yakima gave Annie a hand down. Turning to Beth, Annie said, "It's all right, Beth. He's going to fetch one of those men's horses for us. So we can ride to Hat Creek Station."

Beth didn't say anything. She just stared up at Yakima skeptically.

He booted Wolf on up the creek to where the two dead men's horses—a sorrel and a chestnut—stood idly grazing. They whickered at the stranger's approach, the chestnut sidling away. Yakima swung down from Wolf's back, unsaddled and unbridled the sorrel, turning it loose. It would have to forage on its own. He climbed back atop Wolf and led the chestnut back over to the girls, who were now quietly gathering their blankets and trail possibles.

Yakima adjusted the stirrups to fit Annie then turned to both girls, who stood nearby, holding their sacks and blankets. Annie had a canteen and a small canvas satchel looped over her neck and shoulder. They watched him closely, Beth still appearing a little apprehensive. Annie, however, seemed to have lost her fear of the red-skinned stranger. She regarded him now with an inscrutable little half-smile.

Yakima took their blankets, rolled them together, tied them and strapped them to the back of the chestnut's saddle. He'd already gotten rid of the dead man's blanket roll and his own possibles, not finding anything the girls would want. Both men had been traveling light, their only food a few dried up biscuits and jerky. Grub might have been one of things they'd been looking for when they'd attacked the girls.

One of the things…

When he'd secured the blankets, Yakima tied the three small grubsacks to the saddlehorn. As he did, he glanced over his shoulder at Annie. "Do you have enough food for the ride? Take you most of the day. The Hat Creek Station is roughly twenty miles straight west of here."

"I know where it is," Annie said. "We came through there when we rode the stage down from Cannonball, after Ma married Mister Henricks."

"How 'bout food?"

"There's enough to last the day," Annie said.

"Are you sure?"

Annie smiled and nodded. "I'm sure, Mister Henry."

"Yakima."

"What's that?"

"My pa's dead. I'm Yakima." Smiling, he nudged the girl's chin with his thumb and winked. Then sent a flush into her cheeks.

Yakima held his hand out to her. "Let's get you mounted."

Annie gave him her hand. He helped her toe a stirrup

then lifted her up into the saddle.

"How do the stirrups feel?" he asked her.

She moved her feet around in the stirrups then pooched out her lips and nodded. "They feel just fine, Mist...I mean, Yakima," she corrected herself with a smile.

Yakima bent forward to address Beth. "May I help you into the leather, little lady?"

Beth cast her sister a sour look then returned her beetle-browed gaze to Yakima and shrugged a shoulder.

"One, two, three—here we go!" Yakima swung the child up behind her sister and atop the rolled blankets. "How's that feel?"

"All right," Beth said.

"You sure?"

Beth looked away.

Annie turned her head sideways to glance behind her. "Beth, he asked you if you're sure."

"I'm sure!" Beth shot back, addressing her sister's back.

Annie turned to Yakima. "I'm sorry about her. You'd think she'd be more grateful!"

Again, Beth looked away. She was a tough nut to crack. But Yakima didn't blame her. She had good reason to be wary of a stranger and one with Indian blood in him, to boot. If most people on the plains hadn't experienced their own Indian trouble, they'd certainly heard ample horror stories about those who had.

"That's all right," Yakima said, turning the horse to point it straight west. Stepping back, he said, "All right, now—farewell, you two."

"Continuing north?" Annie asked him.

"That's right."

She nodded, a vaguely disappointed cast to her eyes.

"Why do you ask?" Yakima prodded her.

"Oh, I don't know. I just thought maybe you were going to ride along with us to the Hat Creek Station."

"Annie!" exclaimed Beth, and rammed her fist against her sister's back.

"Beth, I declare—what's got into you?"

"You know what Pa always said—the only good Injun's a—"

"Beth! You hush this instant!"

"Oh, come on, Beth," Yakima said, chuckling. "I done told you I'm only *half* Injun. The other half is white. I got *some* good in me."

"Yakima, I do apologize. Beth is a silly, foul-mouthed child. Tonight, I'm going to wash her mouth out with—"

"Oh, no you ain't!" Beth returned, and punched Annie in the back again.

"Beth, good Lord—what an embarrassment you are!" Annie said over her shoulder, exasperated.

"Just because you've gone all calf-eyed over this Injun

don't mean I have to!"

Annie shuttled her gaze to Yakima, deeply flushing.

Yakima laughed and backed away, holding up his hands palms out. "That's all right, that's all right. Ladies, I will bid you another farewell." He looked at Annie and added soberly, "Good luck to you both and please be careful."

Her face the color of a rose in full bloom, Annie cast her little sister a hateful glare then gigged the chestnut forward, saying over her shoulder, this time to Yakima, "Thank you, Yakima. Farewell to you, too. I hope we can meet again sometime, under better circumstances, so Beth and I can repay you for your help."

"Calf eyes! Calf eyes!" Beth screeched at her sister.

Yakima laughed again, watching the two quarreling girls ride away together.

He stood there, watching them for a long time. Longer than he'd intended to. Longer than he wanted to. What he wanted to do was forget about them and get back to the tending of his own affairs.

Unfortunately, the two girls were stuck in his craw.

It didn't help that as they rode away across the fawn-colored prairie, tracing a course between the broadly scattered bluffs, the prairie and the big bowl of faultless blue morning sky seemed to yawn wide and consume them whole.

Gradually, they were absorbed by all that distance,

having dwindled to a small brown splotch before disappearing altogether.

Forget them, he told himself. *They're not your responsibility. You made a promise to a dying friend. That is your responsibility. You can't be held responsible for every kid with a run of hard luck. There are lots of kids with runs of hard luck. Hell, you were one of them yourself.*

Yakima continued to stare after the girls for a time, feeling an aching in his guts. Finally, with a weary sigh, he climbed into the saddle and booted Wolf north. He kept the horse to a spanking trot for the first couple of miles then eased him into a lope.

He had a lot of ground to cover and not much time to do it in. Not if he didn't want to get trapped by another Plains winter.

He rode over a broad a prairie swell, then another. He rode around the shoulder of a haystack butte. Ten minutes later he rode back around the butte from the north, backtracking. He swung Wolf to his right and booted him West. After about twenty minutes, he spotted the girls ahead of him, once again looking almost profanely small and vulnerable, the fifteen-year-old and the child riding together on the single mount, the vast prairie and the sky stretched out around and above them.

He caught up to them fifteen minutes later, slowing Wolf to a walk as he rode up beside them. They hadn't heard his approach. They jerked frightened gazes at him, eyes widening in shock and then relief. Even Beth's eyes showed relief.

"Yakima!" Annie said, her pretty face shaded by the brim of her floppy felt hat, her blond hair bouncing on her shoulders. She smiled broadly.

"Happy now?" Beth asked her, sneering, though a faint smile tugged at her mouth corners as she glanced at Yakima riding beside them. Riding alone out here with only her sister, she must have felt as vulnerable as she'd looked from Yakima's vantage, so that even a savage half-breed was welcome company.

Yakima pinched his hat brim to the girls then rode ahead, leading the way.

Chapter 10

The Hat Creek Station lay at the base of a pine-stippled bluff in otherwise remote and empty country. The Cheyenne-Black Hills stagecoach trail slithered through that country from the north to continue on past the station to the southwest. The station, once a cavalry outpost erected and garrisoned to help keep settlers out of the Black Hills until the government's treaty with the Sioux was broken, was one of the widely spaced station beads on the long, meandering necklace of the trail.

The station's main building lay on the trail's right side—a barrack-like, two-story log affair with a mansard roof and deeply recessed glass windows. A log barn, two stables and several corrals lay on the opposite side of the trail, flanked by dusty cottonwoods in full autumn gold now as Yakima and the two girls rode into the yard late in the day, the westward angling sun casting long, cool blue shadows. Fallen leaves blew around the yard and the horses' feet as Yakima and the girls put their mounts up to one of the three hitchracks fronting the main building.

A dozen saddled horses stood at the rack to Yakima's left; Yakima noted rifles jutting from most of the scabbards. Two dusty freight wagons were parked to the left of the hitchracks; the four dusty, sweat-lathered mules hitched to each desultorily switched their tails at flies.

Annie swung her right foot over her saddle horn and dropped lithely to the ground then reached up to help her sister down. As she did, she eyed the building speculatively. She glanced at Yakima and said, "Right tidy. I bet it's not a half bad place to work."

Yakima regarded it also, glancing at the horses again and feeling an uneasiness in his belly. "I reckon we'll find out. Come on, ladies—supper's on me."

"You don't have to do that, Yakima," Annie said, holding Beth's hand as the girls mounted the porch steps behind him. "We came here to work, not eat."

"Well, I for one am hungry," Beth said, crankily.

"See there?" Yakima said. "Beth's hungry. And I am, too."

When they'd gained the porch, Yakima stopped and glanced over his shoulder at Annie. "You two wait here. Let me go in and get the lay of the land."

Annie looked up at him, wrinkling the skin above

the bridge of her nose. Beth looked up at her, frowning also, then returned her gaze to Yakima, saying nothing.

Yakima unholstered his stag-gripped forty-four, flicked open the loading gate and filled the chamber he usually kept empty beneath the hammer with a shell from his cartridge belt.

"What's that for?" Annie asked, her voice gravely quiet.

"Insurance."

Yakima spun the cylinder, dropped the hogleg back into its holster and pushed through the heavy batwing doors. He stepped to one side, into the shadow cast by the wall behind him, and stood casting his gaze around.

The room before him was large, cavern-like. The elaborate bar and back bar lay at the far end of the room. It was L-shaped, running along part of the wall to his left, as well. The polished mirrors set in the back bar glistened with the salmon light pushing through the room's several, large windows and reflecting the images of the burly patrons drinking and eating, playing cards and conversing, some laughing.

Five steps rose to Yakima's right, to a raised room where there appeared a few gambling tables and a roulette wheel. Several men sat up there, playing poker. A couple of scantily clad girls sat among them, leaning close to the men, smiling and whispering seductively and fawning over the pasteboards in the men's hands.

Several of the men in the room before Yakima had seen him walk in. Their eyes held on him, scrutinizing him closely, curiously, elbowing others to direct their attention toward the half-breed, as well. The conversational hum in this section of the road ranch lowered considerably, and noticeably, directing the attention of the card players in the raised room to the newcomer, as well.

Most of the men returned their attention to their drinks and conversation as well as to the pasteboards in their hands. Likes blacks, Mexicans and Orientals, men of obviously mixed heritage were not an uncommon sight on the frontier West. Mostly of only passing interest. Yakima tended to attract more attention because he was a big, muscular man, with striking green eyes and he wore a gun. The combination of his having Indian blood as well as being large and imposing of stature, tended to attract more attention than he would have liked.

Some men found him threatening or antagonizing—a half-breed wearing a tied-down gun and a bowie knife, a handsome Winchester in his saddle scabbard. Obviously, a gunslinger. A half-breed gunslinger.

Who in the hell did the breed think he was?

More than a few eyes lingered on Yakima. Mostly, however, the clientele returned to their drinks, conversation, and poker. When he was sure that none of the eyes remaining on him were overtly or imminently threatening, he glanced over the batwings at Annie and Beth. He drew one of the batwings open with his gloved hand and jerked his head for the pair to enter, which they did, Annie holding Beth's hand.

"Come on," he said, and led the pair toward one of the room's handful of empty tables.

A serving girl had just finished cleaning off the table and now she stood nearby, gazing with interest at the big half-breed sauntering toward her with two girls in two, one not as big as one of Yakima's buckskin clad legs. Of course, the girls had attracted the room's attention again, but none of it seemed threatening though Yakima leading the two white girls into the road ranch must have amused a few men, for he noted chuckles and laughter from various points around the room.

He ignored it and kicked out a chair.

The serving girl, in her early twenties and wearing a frilly satin gown and with matching feathers in her dark-red hair, red paint on her plump lips and much rouge on her pale cheeks, took in Beth and Annie and then looked back at Yakima and said, "Well, well...what have we here?"

"Prospective employees," Yakima told the girl, helping little Beth into the chair he'd just kicked out. "Could we get one beer and two sarsaparillas and maybe a little conversation with whoever does the hiring around here? We'd like to order supper, too."

The girl arched her copper brow. "Prospective employees, eh? All three of you?" She raked her lusty gaze across Yakima's broad chest and shoulders then returned her gaze to his face and smiled.

"Just the girls. They came from a bad situation and need a place to stay. They're both willing to work to earn their keep."

"Even the little one?"

"Even the little one," Beth said, holding her chin resolutely high, her arms crossed on the edge of the table before her.

"Well, well…" the serving girl trilled, and flounced away.

When the redhead returned, she was accompanied by a lean man in a soiled apron with a craggy face adorned by a handlebar mustache. He had a cigarette dangling from one corner of his mouth.

"All three of 'em?" he asked he redhead.

"Just the girls, not the breed," the serving girl said as she set a mug of sudsy ale on the table in front of Yakima.

"Hell, I could use you at night," the aproned gent said to Yakima. "I need a bouncer. A fella your size. What do you say? I'll pay you fifty cents a night. During the day, you can work in the barn. Do you know hor—?"

"Just the girls," Yakima said.

"Who are they?" the man said scrutinizing each girl

in turn.

Annie told the man her story.

"Ah, hell—that Wayne Henricks is a nasty SOB, if you'll pardon my French, little lady. Your ma should a never married that rascal. I'll see what I can do for you." The apron shifted his gaze to Beth. "As for you—can you wash dishes? I had a Chinaman quit on me two nights ago. Went up to Deadwood to dig for gold, he told me." The apron looked at Yakima and chuckled. "Can you imagine a Chinaman diggin' for gold?"

He chuckled again.

Yakima sipped his beer.

"I can wash all the dishes you need washed," Beth said, adding haughtily, "for the right price."

The apron chuckled again. "I'll tell you the right price—ten cents a day and free room and board. You work the noon lunch and all night as folks is eating. Can you do that?"

Yakima winced. That was a lot of hard work for a girl Beth's age.

"I can do all that and more!" Beth said, sitting back in her chair and crossing her arms on her chest.

"What about me?" Annie asked the man.

The man looked at her, scrutinized her closely, turning his head this way and that.

"All right," he said, knocking on the table once then

walking away, adding, "we'll see about you."

When the man had left, the redhead stepped up to take Yakima and the girls' orders. The special was fried chicken with potatoes and milk gravy, so they ordered that and a big piece of apple pie with whipped cream for dessert. According to a placard on the table, the pie was an extra twelve cents. It was a luxury Yakima could ill afford, but he wanted to indulge these girls. They'd been indulged damned little of late and likely wouldn't be indulged again for quite some time. He still had a small stake in his boot from his job as town marshal down in Apache Springs.

He wasn't sure how he was going to get through the winter, but he'd cross that bridge when he came to it. Maybe find a deputy town marshal's job in Kansas or back down in New Mexico. He sure as hell hoped he made it out of Dakota before the snow flew. This little side trip with Annie and Beth was a delay he could not afford. It was also one he had not been able to avoid.

He hoped things worked out for the girls here. He couldn't help worrying about them both, not at all liking the image he had in his mind of either girl's future working here in such a roughhewn place.

But, then, what other options did they have?

The chicken came and all three ate with relish. Annie and Beth were so hungry they nearly finished their pie at the same time Yakima did. Beth dropped her fork on her plate, looked across the table at her sister, and belched.

"Beth, your manners!"

Beth stuck her tongue out at her sister.

Before Annie could respond, the apron walked up and dropped what appeared at first glance a scrap of frilly pink cloth on the table, some of it so sheer that Yakima could see the scarred tabletop through it.

"Go on upstairs and put that on and let me see you in it. If you look all right, you got a job!"

Both Annie and Beth stared down in wide-eyed shock at what Yakima now saw was a corset and bustier.

"Hold on," Yakima told the apron.

The man frowned. "What?"

"She's not workin' upstairs. Giver her something in the kitchen."

"What're you talkin' about—'give her somethin' in the kitchen'? Look at her. She's filled out right nice…in all the right places…and she's young. I'm guessin' not sixteen yet. Probably fifteen? Don't matter—we'll say you're fourteen and make twice as much—"

"Give her somethin' in the kitchen," Yakima repeated, tightening his voice and hardening his jade eyes. "She's not working the line."

"I don't need nobody else in the kitchen. I have enough cooks, even servin' girls. What I need is—"

"It's all right, Yakima." Annie had set her right hand down on the little garment on the table before her and looked up resignedly at her half-breed benefactor. "I sort of knew that…well…I'd have to do somethin' like this. Not many options for a girl my age."

"No, Annie," Yakima and Beth said at the same time.

Annie took the corset and bustier in both hands and held it up in front of her. "I can try it for a few months, maybe a year. Leastways, I'll try it on, see how I—"

Yakima leaned forward, his voice commanding. "No! I've known women who've worked the line. Married one of 'em. Working the line killed her even long after she quit it."

Annie frowned with concern. "I'm sorry…"

Still standing at the table, arms crossed on his chest, the apron puffed his cigarette and said, "Look, if you want to work here, you're gonna have to try that on. Otherwise…" He threw his hands up.

Keeping her eyes on Yakima, Annie started to rise, the skimpy garment in her hand. "I'll just go up and…"

Yakima slapped the table. "No, you're not."

A loud ringing rose from up near the front of the room. Yakima looked that way to see an unshaven, unwashed saddle tramp rattling a spoon against an empty beer schooner. He sat with four others of the same ilk—dirty, greasy, likely smelly, and ugly to boot. Small time outlaws. Likely stock thieves. They probably belonged to the horses to which saddle scabbards were strapped.

When the room fell silent, the greasy saddle tramp set down the spoon. He was grinning heavy-lidded toward Yakima.

"What the hell was all that racket about, Shamus?" the apron asked.

Shamus's lusty gaze was now on Annie. "I say let her try it on!"

"Yeah," said another man sitting with Shamus. He was big, bald, and bearded. "Let us be the judge if she stays or goes."

The apron held his hands up. "Now, fellas…just stay out of this."

"Go to hell, Murphy," the bald man barked before shuttling his gaze back to Yakima. "Stay out of the girls' business, breed. And while you're at it, get the hell out of here. I for one don't much care for dinin' in the same room as a stinking half-breed son of a bitch!"

Chapter 11

The four other saddle tramps laughed raucously at the big man's rage. They were all glassy-eyed drunk and full of pluck. Sweaty, drunk and wind-burned after a long ride from some hole-in-the wall hideout, no doubt.

Yakima tamped down the rage building inside him. This was no time to blow his fuse. He had the two girls to worry about. If lead flew, they'd be in harm's way. In fact, Beth sat directly between him and the five saddle no-accounts. Annie, sitting to his left, would be in the line of fire, as well.

Both girls looked at him. Fear shone in their eyes.

In fact, all eyes in the room were on him again. The men around him stared with expectant smiles, eager for a show, waiting…wondering how he was going to respond to the bald man's affront.

He was wondering the same thing.

The best thing would be for him and the girls to get up and walk out of here. To hell with his pride. His pride wasn't worth endangering the girls.

He was about to do just that when the big bald man gained his feet so suddenly that his chair flew out from behind him to slam against the front wall, beneath one of the large windows flanking him. A low, collective gasp rose from the onlookers. The bald man held his big, ham-like hands over the butts of the two six-shooters holstered on his broad hips, over his patched corduroy trousers.

He flexed his fingers and pulled his chin down, hard eyes boring into Yakima with open challenge.

Big mistake coming in here, the half-breed admonished himself. He should have let the girls make their way here alone. In his company, they were in more danger than they would have been without him. *Fool!*

The room was as quiet as a held breath.

Suddenly, Beth whipped her head around to the bald man, and shrieked, "Stand down, you drunken gutter trash!" The scream rocketed around the room, making everyone leap a little in their chairs.

It even made the bald man jerk with a start.

As snickers and chuckles broke out among the onlookers, the bald man turned his icy glare on Beth, his broad cheeks coloring with embarrassment.

Yakima's heart thudded. *No,* he thought, *don't you do it!*

The thought had no sooner passed over his brain than the bald man, his glare still pinned on the shaver, bunched his crimson cheeks in rage, said, "Why, you little—" and reached for both his pistols at the same time.

Annie screamed, "*Beth!*"

Yakima leaped up out of his chair, his .44 instantly in his right hand, bucking and lapping flames a half a wink before both the bald man's guns spoke, as well. Yakima's bullet punched through the big hellion's chest, puffing dust from his shirt and nudging both the man's slugs wide of Beth. One ricochetted off a potbelly stove just beyond her; the other thumped into the backbar mirror with a shriek of breaking glass and evoking a bellowing wail from the apron.

The bald man wailed, as well, as the bullet punched him backward and through the window behind him with a second, louder shriek of breaking glass.

For two or three stretched seconds, everyone in the room stared at the broken window where the bald man's right boot had gotten hung up on the sill so that the badly scuffed sole, showing the man's grimy white sock through a quarter-sized hole, faced the room.

The four men sitting at the bald man's table stared at the boot.

Then they swung their heads slowly toward Yakima, eyes wide and spitting fire.

"*Beth!*" Annie screamed again and threw herself out of her chair and into her sister, driving little Beth to the floor and covering the child with her body.

At nearly the same time, the ragged saddle tramp who'd rattled his spoon against his beer schooner leaped up out of his chair, slapping leather. At nearly the same time, the one sitting to the right of the bald man's empty chair leaped out of his own chair, also clawing iron.

Bang! Bang!

Both men screamed as Yakima's bullets cut into them, one firing his Colt into the ceiling above his head, the second firing his Remington into the round table before him, scattering cards and coins. The last two were already on their feet as Yakima punched the tickets of the first two, one getting off a shot that also broke the back bar mirror behind Yakima (and evoking another wail from the apron cowing on the floor in front of the bar) just before Yakima drilled a round through the man's left cheek, sending him stumbling backward against the wall with a walleyed look on his badly sunburned, blond-mustached face.

The fourth man got off a shot, as well, the bullet ripping across the outside of Yakima's right arm just as Yakima quickly but calmly lined up his sights on the man's chest and triggered a fifth round. The bullet punched through the man's breastbone, evoking a howl and sending him flying through the window to the right of the first one, blood spurting from the hole in his chest.

Again, silence fell over the room. It was like a hot, wet blanket. All eyes shuttled from the two broken windows and the dead man leaning back against the wall between them with his head tipped back, eyes rolled back in his head, to Yakima.

Firmly, still holding his cocked Colt straight out from his right shoulder, Yakima glanced down at Annie still lying on the floor over her sister, and said, "Annie—get Beth outside. Mount up."

Annie turned her head to look up at him. "What about you?"

Yakima looked around the room for another threat, shifting the Colt along with his gaze. "I'll be along."

Annie rose quickly and drew Beth to her feet. Both girls looked pale, eyes round with shock as they looked around the room that was so silent you could have heard a pin drop.

"Hurry," Yakima said.

Annie took Beth's hand and led her quickly across the room and out the batwings. When the girls were clear, Yakima followed, moving slowly, wending his way through the tables, swinging his gaze and the Colt all around him, wary of a shot from behind. Every man and woman in the place sat still as statues. All except the apron who, as Yakima gained the batwings, rose heavily and glanced at his broken back bar mirror and two broken windows. He turned to Yakima and yelled, "You owe me for three chicken dinners, two broke windows and a busted mirror, *redskin!*"

Yakima turned to the man, pulled a gold piece out of his buckskins pocket, and tossed it. The apron caught it one handed and looked at it.

"That's only ten dollars!"

"As for the rest," Yakima said, "you can go to hell!"

He backed through the doors and continued backing across the porch. At the top of the steps, he turned, leaped to the ground and hurried over to rip Wolf's reins from the hitchrack. Annie had lifted Beth atop the chestnut and had just toed a stirrup. Yakima walked over to her, swung her up into the saddle then stepped into his own.

"Can you gallop?" he asked Annie.

"Watch me." Annie turned her head to one side and said to her sister, "Hold on tight, Beth!"

She batted her heels against the chestnut's flanks. Yakima was impressed to see both girls stay on as the horse lunged suddenly off its rear hooves and stretch into a hard run to the north. They both leaned far forward, Beth pressing her cheek against her sister's back, arms wrapped tightly around Annie's waist. Yakima booted Wolf into a run, as well and they left a thick fog of dust sifting down over the yard of the Hat Creek Station, which was still as quiet as a parlor house on a Sunday morning.

He doubted any of the clientele would try to run him down, but since he'd suddenly found himself playing mother hen to two girls, he wasn't going to take any chances.

He and they rode hard for a good mile and then Yakima slowed Wolf to a walk. Annie slowed the chestnut then, as well. She glanced over her shoulder in the direction of the road ranch, then turned to Yakima, a question in her still fear-bright eyes.

She didn't have to ask it. *What now?*

Yeah, he thought, what now?

Annie glanced at his arm, saw the blood. "Yakima, you're hit!"

He glanced at the bloody tear in his right shirt sleeve. "Just a scratch. It can wait." He glanced at the sun hanging low in the west. "Sundown soon. We'd best find a place to camp."

They rode up and over a jog of low hills. Yakima led the girls off the trail to the east for nearly a mile. He wanted to get a good way off the trail. When he came to a creek, he led the girls across it to a horseshoe bend on the opposite side. Large cottonwoods grew along the base, offering good cover.

He unsaddled Wolf close enough to the stream that the horse could drink at will, fed him some cracked corn and rubbed him down with a scrap of burlap. He watched as the girls tended their own horse. They did so automatically without having to be told. They worked silently, both a little pale with the shock of what they'd seen.

When Yakima had tied both mounts to a picket pin, he told the girls to gather wood for a fire then knelt beside the stream and removed his shirt. He crouched over the water and cupped the cool liquid to the ragged gash on his arm.

He heard Annie say something to Beth; she said it so quietly that he couldn't make out the words. Footsteps sounded behind him and then Annie knelt beside him.

"Let me help you," she said. She held a small canvas pouch in her hand.

"I got it. Like I said, just a scratch."

Annie studied him closely from below his right shoulder, looking up at him timidly. She didn't say anything for a full minute. Then she said, "Yakima, are you mad at us? Beth's sorry for losing her temper in there."

Yakima looked at her, one brow arched in surprise. "Mad at *you?* Hell, no! Not the shaver, neither. Beth was just bein' Beth!" Remembering the younger girl's screeching tirade in the station house, Yakima chuckled as he continued cupping water to his arm. "If I'm mad at anyone, I'm mad at me. Damn stupid for me to ride in there with you. I was the one who brought the trouble.

You didn't have a chance with me ridin' shotgun!"

He wagged his head in frustration then gritted his teeth at the burn of the cold water against the fresh wound.

"If we'd ridden in there alone, we'd likely still be there," Annie said quietly, keeping her grave eyes on his.

"That'd be your decision. I've got no right to tell you what to do. Doing so, I nearly got you and Beth killed. Only now…what in holy blazes am I gonna do with the two of you?"

Annie leaned close to study the wound, saying forlornly, "I reckon we're all alone, Beth an' me. It's better than living with Mister Henricks. We have no one but our grandparents up in Cannonball but it's a far piece and there's no tellin' if they'd take us in or not. They're notional, as Ma used to say." She looked up at him. "I can sew that wound shut for you. Ma taught me on account of doctors bein' too expensive for such simple things as suturing a cut."

Yakima glanced at his arm, shook his head. "No need. It's not deep. It'll heal on its own."

"Let me put some salve on it, at least."

"All right."

As she pulled a small tin from the bag, removed the lid and gently rubbed the salve into the ragged, shallow trough that ran for roughly two inches across the outside of his arm, Yakima gazed at the girl, a crosshatch of deep lines cutting across his copper forehead. What, indeed, was he going to do with the pair?

He glanced over to where little Beth was gathering sticks and branches off the ground around the cottonwoods. Moving stiffly, almost as though she were in a trance, she cradled the sticks she'd already picked up in one arm, reaching down with her small, free hand to gather more, her gray wool skirt swishing around her legs. Her old, dark-red coat was coated with bits of bark and leaves. She wore no hat and her brown hair blew around her head in the wind.

She didn't show it openly, but Yakima sensed the fear in the child. He sensed the fear in Annie, too. They were strong kids. They'd been through a lot and that made you strong. Yakima knew that from his own experience. Still, they were afraid of what might lie ahead for them.

Strong as he was and a full-grown man, Yakima knew something about that fear, as well. He felt it in the night, usually deep in the night, after his fire had burned down to smoking gray ashes and he found himself alone in the darkness.

Annie finished rubbing the salve into the wound and looked up at Yakima, scraping the last of the salve from her finger on the edge of the tin. "It's wintergreen and shadbark root. Ma's own family recipe for staving off infection."

"I reckon we're going to Cannonball," Yakima blurted out before he'd fully realized what he'd been going to say.

He didn't like the sound of it at all. Cannonball was out of his way. It was nearly straight north, along the old Bismarck-Deadwood stage line. He was headed northeast. The detour would delay his arriving at Fort Abercrombie by a good week. He was liable to get stuck for the winter up there. Also, it would be a dangerous journey through perilous country. North of Deadwood was still wild country—outlaw and Indian country.

Most of the Indians had been hazed onto reservations, but there were many wild bands still running free. Their ill-treatment by whites had turned them savage and vengeance hungry. While Yakima didn't blame them one bit for not wanting to be herded and confined like cattle, the fact that several bands of Sioux and Cheyenne still ran wild between Deadwood and Bismarck was something to consider.

Even if Yakima and the girls made it one piece to Cannonball, there were no guarantees that the girls' grandparents could or would take them in.

It must have sounded far better to Annie than it did to him.

As she gazed up at him, her dour features blossomed into a full-blown smile, blue eyes sparkling like candles on Christmas eve. She threw her arms around Yakima, hugging him, pressing her cheek against his chest and yelling, "Oh, Beth—we're going to Cannonball!"

Chapter 12

The next morning, at dawn's first blush, Yakima roused the girls.

At least, he roused Annie but when he placed his hand on Beth's shoulder to give her a gentle shake, she merely grumbled and turned over on her belly.

"Oh, Beth—no," Annie said.

"Come on, honey," Yakima said, giving the girl another gentle shake.

Beth just grunted and pulled her blankets up over her head.

Yakima looked at Annie who'd been rolling her own blankets but who now knelt beside her sister, staring down at Beth with concern. To Yakima, she said, "She gets this way. She got like this after Ma died...not wanting to get out of bed in the morning. Mister Henricks threatened to whip her. That didn't help."

Annie leaned forward and touched her sister's shoulder through the blankets. "Beth, come on—you have to get up. It's morning. We have to get an early start. It's a long ride to Cannonball."

"No!"

Yakima said, "Let's give her a few minutes. I'll build the fire up, get it a little warmer. It's a chilly mornin'."

Yakima had started a fire after he himself had risen. Now he added a couple of stout branches, building up the flames. He filled a coffee pot from the creek and set it to boil while Annie fried sowbelly and corncakes. When the water for the coffee came to a boil, Annie added the Arbuckles, brought it to a boil once more, added a little cold water to settle the grounds, then poured two cups of coffee and brought one over to where he was saddling both horses.

"Is she up yet?" he asked, accepting the steaming cup from Annie, who wore her wool coat and her hat pulled down over her ears against the cold.

"No."

"I thought she'd get up when she smelled the food."

"I did, too. I'll try to rouse her again."

Yakima was working on the girl's horse when he heard a shrill: "No! Leave me alone! I ain't goin' anywhere!"

He glanced over the chestnut's back to see Annie kneeling over Beth, a helpless expression on the older girl's face.

"Please, Beth, you have to get up. We're going to see Gramps and Grandma!" Annie said as Yakima continued rigging the girls' horse.

"I don't wanna see Gramps and Grandma! They only like you! They don't like me! You're nice and you're pretty! I'm mean and ugly!" Yakima looked up to see the smaller girl sitting up now, knees raised to her chest, arms wrapped around them, over her blanket, bawling. "I want Ma! I want Pa! I want everything to be just like it *used to be!*"

"Well, it can't be that way, Beth! Come on, now—get up!" Annie tugged on Beth's right arm. "Yakima's waitin' on us! You have to eat and we have to go!"

Finished with the chestnut, Yakima walked around behind the horse and back into the camp. He walked up to where Annie stood over Beth, holding the little girl's wrist in her hand and gazing down at her in frustration.

She looked up at Yakima and said, "I'm sorry, Yakima. I never know what to do with her when she gets like this."

Yakima dropped to a knee and placed his hand gently over the back of the sobbing child's head. "We all get like this from time to time. We just want everything to go back to the way it was. We want everybody we love to be alive again. And happy. To be with us forever."

He closed his hand soothingly over the back of Beth's head, running his fingers through her thin brown hair.

"It takes all the starch out of us to know that that's never gonna happen. Some days we don't want to get up and face the world. We just want the world to go away and leave us alone."

Beth lifted her head and looked at Yakima through tear-drenched eyes. "Even you?"

Yakima nodded. "You see, there was a woman I loved. She died in my arms, oh…five, six years ago now in Colorado. It seems like only yesterday she was alive and we were happy and in love and ranching together in Arizona, planning a family. That she's gone and we'll never be together again and we'll never have that family we wanted so much just sticks in my craw somethin' awful. All the damn time. Never goes away."

A tear leaked out of his right eye and dribbled down his cheek. He was surprised that he didn't brush it away but just left it there for the girls to see.

He smiled but his voice broke as he said, "But I'll never have her again and that's just the way it is. But I know she's looking down on me, still loving me and wishing me the best without her and that she wants me to keep rolling out of the old mattress sack every morning no matter how much I don't want to…and to pull my boots on and to mount ol' Wolf and ride. To put one foot in front of the other. To make somethin' out of this life as long I'm still on this side of the sod."

Yakima paused. Both girls were crying now, staring at him, tears dribbling down their cheeks like summer rain down windows. Yakima sandwiched Beth's face in his big hands and swabbed her tears with his thumbs. "You understand now, Beth? You're not alone. We're all in this together."

Lips quivering and the tears still flowing, Beth nodded and threw her arms around Yakima and pressed her wet face against his throat.

Annie drew in and wrapped an arm around each of them and they sobbed together for a good, long time.

***

The day heated up quickly and by noon the three had taken off their coats and tied them around their blanket rolls. It heated up even more after noon so that by four o'clock and maybe forty miles north of where they'd camped the previous night, Yakima glanced over at the two girls keeping pace behind him.

They were following an old Indian trail he'd taken previously on trips through the Dakota and Wyoming Territories, avoiding settlements and main trails and the trouble they inevitably entailed.

Both girls were sunburned and weary-looking, Annie crouched forward over her saddle horn. Riding behind her, Beth canted her head to see around her sister. She looked just as hot and sunburned and trail weary as Annie. Sweat streaked the trail dust on both girls' faces. Their blouses and dresses clung to their sweaty bodies; their hair was pasted to their cheeks.

"Ladies, it's getting late. It's been a long and weary day, I know"—he cracked a reassuring smile—"but just up yonder you're gonna be in for a real treat."

He canted his head toward the top of the mesa they were climbing. At the mesa's crest, sloping like a ship's prow, lay a thick fringe of pines, firs and cedars as well as a few autumn-gold aspens. Just on the other side of those trees was a rocky sandstone dike that resembled the finned back of some dinosaur carcass half buried in the mountain.

"What's up yonder?" Annie asked, wrinkling the skin above the bridge of her red-mottled nose.

"Follow me and you will see!" Yakima thrust his arm forward and continued walking Wolf on up the sloping mesa.

When they reached the crest of the mesa, the girls followed Yakima and Wolf through the pines and aspens. The air was a little cooler here, fragrant with the fallen aspen leaves and pine sap. Yakima continued leading the pair along the base of the dike until they came to a crack, or a stone corridor, that cut through it.

When they'd ridden thirty or forty yards through the corridor, the floor began to slope downwards, both stone corridors falling away behind them. They continued down through more pines, cedars and aspens. They dropped maybe a hundred feet before Yakima reined up on a stone ledge. He turned to the girls as Annie halted the chestnut to his right and gestured toward the cool, dark, sunlit water of a stream meandering through its cut maybe fifty feet below the ledge.

"Ladies, I give you the White River."

"Beautiful!" said Annie.

"Wow!" said Beth. She looked hopefully at Yakima. "Can we go swimmin'? I'm as hot and stinky as an old bull buff!"

Yakima gestured toward a curve in the creek upstream to his left. The curve formed a pool shaded by the high, ribbed, sandstone ledge rising on the other side and also studded with cedars.

"That there is my own private swimmin' hole. Every time I've ridden through here, I've stopped to swim. Less'n it was winter, of course. I'm sure it was a private swimmin' hole of an Indian or two who once lived around here, but for right now I consider it my own private hole."

Annie smiled and arched her brows. "Will you share it with us, Yakima?"

Yakima grinned broadly and winked. "Follow me,

ladies!"

They followed the trail—still the ancient Indian trail—down the steep slope, weaving amongst the trees. Yakima halted Wolf on the stream's stone bank, swung down from the saddle, pulled the saddle off and turned to the girls, grinning broadly. "Last one in's a rotten egg!"

He walked over to the chestnut and helped the girls off the mount's back.

"I'll take care of your horse," Yakima told Annie, and canted his head at the inky dark, inviting stream reflecting the late afternoon's golden sunlight. "You an' Beth go swimmin', have some fun."

"I reckon you're gonna be the rotten egg, then, Yakima," Beth accused him with a cute little smirk.

"I been a rotten egg my whole life—why stop now?" he said as he loosened the chestnut's saddle cinch.

While Beth unbuttoned her coat as she walked over to some shrubs lining the riverbank, Annie walked over to Yakima, placed a hand on his shoulder, rose onto her toes and planted a tender kiss on his right cheek. "I happen to know you're not rotten at all." She winked then flounced off behind shrubs near Beth to disrobe.

Yakima chuckled as he stripped the gear from the chestnut, which wandered a little way down the trail, near where Wolf stood stomping in happy relief to be free of his leather, to a relatively flat area carpeted in ferns. The chestnut lay down and rolled. Wolf nosed the gelding then put his head down before lifting it sharply up again and gave a frisky whinny.

Both horses hurried down the slope to drink in the stream.

"Don't look—we're comin' out!" Beth called as Yakima arranged his and the girl's gear in a little clearing several yards back from the stream and which he'd deemed a good place to camp for the night. They wouldn't be far from the trail, but he'd taken the trail many times over the years and he'd seen few signs of anyone else having traveled it at all.

"I ain't lookin'," Yakima said, glancing up automatically to glimpse both girls hurrying out of the shrubs and down the slope to the water, clad in their white cotton chemises and pantaloons.

"You peeked!" Annie said, casting a quick glance over her shoulder as she followed Beth down the slope.

"Sorry about that—I didn't mean to. Don't worry, I'll scour the image from my head right now!"

"Ah," Annie said, laughing as she cast another look behind her. "You don't have to go that far!" She gave a flirtatious wink and then she and Beth, holding their hands out for balance, their camisoles buffeting around their legs, bare from the knees down, dropped down to the bottom of the slope to test the water.

Yakima chuckled as he continued arranging the gear around the spot where he figured he'd build a fire. Soon, he could hear the girls splashing in the water.

As he gathered deadfalls along the slope and amongst the pines and golden aspens with which to build a fire, Annie called, "Aren't you coming in?"

Chapter 13

Yakima glanced down to where Beth and Annie were treading water several feet out from the sandy shore, Annie a few yards farther out than where Beth was holding her nose and dunking her head.

Yakima shook his head as he dropped an armload of the wood near where he figured to build a fire ring. "Not this time. I'm gonna keep an eye out and build a fire. You two are gonna be cold once you climb out of there."

"Oh, come on!" Annie called, her wet hair pasted against her head and floating in the water around her. "Don't be a spoilsport! Besides, it feels *sooo* good!"

"Yeah—come on in, Yakima! Don't be a spoilsport." Suddenly, Beth frowned with curiosity. "Or...don't you people swim...?"

Annie turned to her sister, aghast. "*What?*"

"I don't know," Beth said. "I reckon I never thought of

an Injun swimmin'.'"

"What?" Yakima said, chuckling as he neatly arranged the deadfall. "You think we're just galloping horses and taking scalps all the time?"

"Yeah, I guess," Beth said, still frowning, deep lines laddering her pale, sunburned forehead.

"Beth!" Annie cried. But then she, too, turned to regard Yakima curiously. "You do swim, don't you, Yakima?"

Yakima laughed. He rose, doffed his hat, kicked out of his boots and unbuckled his cartridge belt, which he coiled neatly and lay atop his saddle. He turned to the girls as he started to unbutton his shirt. "Turn around, now. No peekin'!"

"You peeked at Annie!" Beth returned, customarily defiant.

"That was an accident."

"No, it wasn't. Everybody peeks at Annie"—she turned to Annie, smiling jeeringly— "now after she's all filled out where all the men want their women filled out!" She lifted a hand to her mouth, snickering.

"Beth!" Annie said, using the back of her hand to splash water at her sister. But Yakima could see she was blushing. She glanced up at him, snickered, then, composing herself, said, "Oh, all right—we'll turn around. Turn around, Beth. We don't want to embarrass the poor man."

"I'm just gonna close my eyes," Beth said, squeezing

her eyes shut but keeping her pug nose pointed toward Yakima.

"You don't peek now," Yakima grunted as he stumbled around, shucking out of his pants.

Below him in the river, the girls giggled.

"All right, here I come," Yakima said, throwing his sweaty socks down then tramping barefoot down the slope, his wash-worn longhandles clinging to his brawny, long-legged frame. "Don't you peek!"

"I know Beth is peeking, because that's Beth's way, but I'm not going to because I'm a lady," Annie said superiorly.

Yakima stepped off the gravelly bank and into the water. He walked out until the water rose up over his knees, past Beth and then past Annie, as well, who had her back to him. He lifted his arms, threw them straight out before him and dove forward and under the crisp, cool stream. He felt the soothing pressure of the water scouring away the many days of trail grime from his longhandles and hide, cleaning the sweat from his hair. The water was like the kisses of a thousand gentle lovers.

He surfaced then lowered his head again and swam straight out into the main current. The current wasn't very strong here, so he made it easily all the way across the river to the stone ridge that formed its other side. The ridge was a giant granite monolith towering a hundred feet over the river.

He lifted his head above the water and looked back to see Annie and Beth watching him, smiling.

"You're a show-off, Yakima!" Beth shouted out at him., Annie laughed.

"Show-off, eh? Watch *this!*"Yakima turned to the ridge, found a hold, and hoisted himself up out of the river.

The ridge jutted nearly straight up out of the water, but on one of his past visits here, just for a rare bit of fun, he'd found enough cracks, fissures and crevices to climb it. He climbed it now, quickly, adeptly using his hands and feet, crawling up the nearly sheer rock like a bug climbing a wall.

After so long on his horse, it felt good to use muscles he so seldom used, stretching out his arms as well as his legs. In his late thirties, he was not a young man anymore, but he was pleased to discover that he still had some of the strength and dexterity that his old friend Ralph had found impressive many years ago when they'd laid rails together and drank and gambled at hell-on-wheels every night. They'd practiced Shaolin fighting techniques every Sunday afternoon, usually along the shore of a stream such as this one.

When he'd climbed about fifty feet, he stopped and hoisted himself onto a stone shelf shaped like a tongue poking out over the river. He walked out to the end of the tongue and smiled down at the two girls staring up at him in awe.

He grinned and waved, thoroughly enjoying showing off for the girls.

He cupped his hands around his mouth and yelled, "Dare me to jump?"

"No!" Annie cried, closing both hands over her mouth.

"Jump!" Beth screamed, leaping up and down in the water and splashing with excitement.

"Here goes!"

Yakima stepped out into thin hair.

He heard Annie cry, "Yakima!"

As he dropped, he raised his knees to his chest and wrapped his arms around them. The sun-glinting black surface of the stream grew quickly beneath him. He knew from a previous exploration that a deep pool lay at the base of the stone ridge. He struck the surface with a cannon like sound and the cold water of the pool closed around him as did a peaceful silence save for the sounds of rising bubbles.

He straightened as he descended, struck the pool's stony bottom with both feet. He propelled himself upward with his feet and arms and a few seconds later his head broke the surface. He shook his head wildly, wet hair dancing across his shoulders.

"What a splash!" Beth cried.

Annie faced him, treading water and smiling.

Grinning, Yakima swam toward the girls, taking long forward strokes with his arms, kicking his feet. His heart was light and buoyant. It hadn't felt like that in a long time. Hell, maybe it hadn't felt like that since he'd been a kid running in the woods and swimming and just having fun for the sake of fun. He was grateful that the girls had reminded him of what it was like to be young. They were certainly not care-free, but they were young and maybe he'd just discovered that he was still young at heart.

Or at least that he could be young at heart sometimes.

He would make a mental note of that for later, when times were hard again. Which, of course, they would be. There was no escaping life's problems. But it was good to take a break from them now and then.

He had the girls and their willingness to be entertained to thank for reminding him of that. And for reminding him that he was still a show-off at heart. An over-grown boy still resided inside him though he wasn't allowed out very often.

Annie swam toward him.

"Careful," he said, "the current's a little stronger out here."

She smiled as she swam. "I'm strong. Not as strong as you, but I'm strong."

When she was within four feet of him, she wheeled back in the water, bringing her feet forward, lifting the right one out of the water and lightly splashing him. She smiled playfully, the sunlight glinting off her lilac eyes. Yakima grabbed her ankle and pulled her toward him, laughing.

"Careful, or I'll—"

He stopped when she placed her hands on his face, down around his jaws and slid her face up close to his, gazing at him gravely, her eyes wide and soft. That look in her eyes, so unexpected, took Yakima aback. He just stared at her, not sure what to say. She seemed to want to say something herself but was having as much trouble as he was getting the words out.

Finally, Yakima laughed to defuse the suddenly serious nature of the situation, pulled away from the girl, and said, "Come on, darlin'—we'd best get dried out. Gonna turn cold soon. I'll get a fire started."

"Yakima," she called quietly behind him, her voice low and intimate, vaguely pleading.

No, no, no, he told himself. He ignored her and smiling at Beth, continued swimming toward her and shore. Beth gave him a slit-eyed, accusing look as he approached her.

Yakima chuckled, wrapped his arm around her waist and pulled her along beside him. "Come on, half-pint—I'll race you to shore!"

***

Yakima woke with a grunt. Instantly, his .44 was in his hand. He cocked the hammer and aimed it into the darkness around him.

He'd heard something in his sleep. He didn't know what it was. His ears had only detected a sound and in his experience, sounds could be dangerous.

Now he heard a gasp from the darkness on his left.

"Yakima," Annie called in a hushed voice. "It's Annie."

Yakima's heart slowed. He depressed the Colt's hammer and lowered the gun to his side.

"Damn, girl," he said quietly so he wouldn't awaken Beth, "you ought not to sneak up on a man like that!"

"I'm sorry." Quick footsteps rose from the darkness. Annie's blond-haired silhouette took shape before him and on his left. A sickle moon was low and the stars shone brightly, offering enough light that he could see now as she approached that she had a blanket wrapped tightly around her, against the chill night air. Her hair blew back as she hurried toward him.

"I had trouble finding you," she said, stopping and dropping to a knee beside him. "Why are you sleeping way out here?"

He'd laid his saddle and blanket roll a half-dozen or so yards from the fire. He'd sat up late keeping watch and he hadn't wanted the small fire he'd built to cook supper over and to keep the girls warm to compromise his night vision.

That wasn't the only reason. There was another reason. That other reason was Annie.

Maybe, he silently opined, smelling the youthful, earthy fragrance of the river-cleansed girl beside him, she was the main reason.

"What is it?" Yakima said, returning the .44 to the holster beside him. "What's wrong?"

She tossed her hair back behind her shoulders, a distinctly woman-like gesture. He'd detected a few other woman-like gestures in the girl over the past couple of days. "Nothing's wrong. I couldn't sleep. I thought maybe you weren't asleep yet, either."

"Well, I was, so…"

"Can I sit with you a spell?"

Yakima sighed. He lay back against his saddle and tipped his hat back down over his eyes. "All right. Best not leave Beth alone for long, though."

"She's sound asleep."

"But…"

Annie placed her hand on his arm. "Beth's fine, Yakima." She left her hand on his arm.

He peeked up at her from beneath his hat brim, narrowing one eye. "It's not a good idea."

"You bein' out here."

"Why not?"

"It's just not. I don't want you getting the wrong idea."

"About what?" she asked innocently.

Yakima drew a ragged breath. "Us."

"Oh." She quirked her mouth corners in a knowing half-smile. Another woman-like gesture. "Us."

Neither one said anything for maybe two full minutes. Yakima kept his eyes closed though now and then he opened them to see Annie staring straight out into the darkness. She raised her knees toward her chest and wrapped the blanket around them. Her bare feet shone in the starlight.

Finally, she swallowed and turned to him and said very quietly and intimately, "I'm not wearing anything under this blanket, Yakima."

Chapter 14

Yakima poked his hat up onto his forehead and sat up. "No, honey," he said, shaking his head. "That ain't gonna happen."

"What isn't?"

"You know what."

"Why not?"

"It just ain't—that's all. I'm sorry if I gave you the wrong—"

"Don't you think I'm pretty?"

"Why, you're beautiful, honey."

"You don't like me?"

"You know, Annie, I love both you girls, sure enough. But like a brother, not—"

"Oh, *god!*" she cried. "Like a *brother?*"

She leaped up and, holding the blanket close around her shoulders, ran back in the direction of the camp.

Yakima lowered his head and ran his hands through his hair, tugging at it painfully. "Ah, hell!"

He could still hear Annie sobbing as she ran, grass crackling under her bare feet.

Then Beth's voice: "Annie? Annie? What's *wrong?*"

"Never mind!" Annie cried.

She must have lain down in her blankets and pressed her face against the feed sack she was using as a pillow, because her sobs came muffled from the darkness. Muffled though rife with a girl's misery.

"Where's Yakima?" Beth asked.

"Who *cares?*"

Yakima threw himself back against his saddle and expelled a heavy sigh.

***

Yakima slept fitfully and woke as dawn dropped a milky gray light through the trees and over the river. Morning birds flitted about the branches, piping.

He sat up, removing his hat, scratching his head, and yawning. He remembered last night and looked over toward the camp where the girls slept in the small clearing behind him. In the dim light and because of the trees between him and them, he could see only some gear and part of a rumpled blanket.

A dread touched him. The morning—hell, maybe even the whole day—was bound to be awkward as hell for him and Annie. He felt like an idiot about last night, how he'd handled the whole thing.

Like a *brother?* Had he really said that? He could have laid it on her a little more gently than that! He didn't know what exactly he could have said, but obviously the whole "brother" line had been exactly the wrong thing.

Annie was bound to feel humiliated. Because that's what he'd done. He'd humiliated her. He dreaded facing her as he knew she was probably dreading facing him.

Why couldn't he have met up with a couple of orphaned *boys?* Boys would have been a helluva lot easier than girls.

He lowered his head and scrubbed his knuckles across his scalp, found himself chuckling. Ah, hell. No point in delaying the inevitable.

With a weary groan, he donned his hat, climbed to his feet, wrapped and buckled his .44 and bowie knife around his waist and tied the holster to his thigh. He delayed the inevitable by walking over and checking on the horses which he'd tethered only a few yards away. He strapped feed sacks over the snouts of both, then tramped wearily over to the camp.

Beth was snoring softly, curled up in her blankets on her side. As he walked over to the fire ring mounded with gray ashes, he glanced toward Annie's bedroll, glanced away, then glanced back at the bedroll again. He frowned, his heart quickening. Only Annie's rumpled blankets lay in front of the overturned saddle she'd used as a pillow. Annie herself was gone.

Yakima looked around, heart thudding.

"Annie?" he called softly, not wanting to startle Beth.

He turned to stare off into the trees and called Annie's name again quietly. The only reply was the frenzied morning piping of the birds. If she'd merely wandered off to tend nature, she would have heard him. Unless, of course, she was giving him the silent treatment. Which, he guessed, he couldn't really blame her for.

He walked a few steps out into the trees, looking around, the gradually growing light revealing more and more of the forested slope.

But not Annie.

He called twice more, heart beating even faster.

Had she run away in disgust? Was she *that* broken-hearted?

Or...

He turned toward where the river shone through the trees down the slope about a hundred feet.

"Oh, God, no..." He hurried down the slope, weaving through the trees. His breath rasped worriedly in and out of his lungs.

When the trees fell back behind him as he gained the

river's gravelly shore, he looked into the tendrils of pale fog hovering over the dark, faintly rippling water. He cupped his hands to his mouth and bellowed, "Annie!"

"Over here, Yakima." The girl's mild voice had come from his left.

He whipped his head in that direction. She was swimming maybe thirty feet out from shore, a pale splotch against the dark water, partly obscured by the feather-like fog that almost seemed to be whispering quietly above the water's quiet sucking and gurgling sounds and wavelets lapped against the shore.

Relief touched Yakima, instantly slowing his heart. He drew a deep, relieved breath, and said, "What're you doing out there?"

"What's it look like?" she asked, swimming toward him.

"It looks like you're swimming."

Annie smiled and stopped. She was in water shallow enough that she could stand. The water lapped up high enough on her chest that it hid her breasts from his view, but low enough that he could tell she wasn't wearing a stitch. Against his will and to his chagrin, he felt warmth of the ancient male pull climb into his ears.

She canted her head to one side and smiled again. "Want to come in? The water's great."

"Ain't it cold?"

"It's refreshing."

"I...see."

She splayed her hands out on the surface of the water to each side of her, looked at them, and then at Yakima standing on the shore. "I'm sorry about last night."

"I was going to say the same thing."

"No need. You were just being honest."

Yakima sighed and squatted on his haunches, absently scooping up a handful of gravel. "No, I wasn't. Not really. The truth is I had a hard time resisting you last night, young lady, but I had to for both of us."

Annie frowned and again canted her head to one side. "I don't understand. I wanted you to be my first."

"I'm pushing forty years old, Annie. You're a beautiful young woman. You're also feeling lonely and vulnerable. You and me would have been a mistake. Maybe you wouldn't have realized it till later, but eventually you would have. I didn't want to be your first mistake."

"I love you, Yakima."

Yakima shook his head as he let the pebbles dribble slowly out of his hand. "You just think you do. You wait for a young man to come along. A man closer to your own age. He'll be the right one. Me? I'm old enough to be your father, which means I'd have been the wrong one. I know you don't see it that way now. But trust me on this, pretty lady—someday you will."

She pursed her lips and beetled her brows, nodding thoughtfully.

"I want to be a good memory," Yakima said and winked at her. "Not a bad one."

She gave a thin, sad smile.

"So…you forgive me?" he asked her.

She smiled more broadly and nodded. "Forgiven."

"All right, then. Climb on out of there. Let's go wake your sister and get some grub on the fire for breakfast!"

Annie began walking toward shore, the water line dropping quickly down her chest.

"Hold on—not that fast!" Yakima wheeled and hurried up the slope, taking long strides and denying his urge to cast one brief glance back over his shoulder.

Behind him, Annie called, "Chicken!" and laughed.

***

Two days later, Yakima stopped Wolf on Forest Hill and gazed down into Deadwood Gulch. As Annie drew the chestnut up beside him and peered down into the town that filled up the winding gulch below, she turned to Yakima and frowned.

"Why are you shaking your head?"

Yakima glanced at her then turned to stare down into the gulch again. "Last time I was through here—two, maybe three years ago—the town was half this size. Now there's several main thoroughfares and a good many big, brick buildings, just like Denver and Cheyenne! Still a few wooden buildings, but, my god, Deadwood is still roarin'!"

He stared down at the back of an unpainted, three-story, wood-frame building standing maybe a hundred yards out from the base of the ridge that he and the girls were on. Three or four young ladies clad mostly in underwear were sitting on the building's third-floor back porch—if you could call it a porch.

It was the flat roof over a second-floor rear extension. It had no railings. It was furnished with several wash tubs and a line for drying clothes. One of the young doxies was just then smoking a cigarette and hanging wash from a wooden tub on the line while the three others lounged around in chairs, idling away the afternoon until the usual party would begin around five, when the miners would surface from the mines and were ready, by god, to roar!

"Now you're smiling," Annie observed. She frowned and canted her head to one side as she asked with a ring of good-natured admonishment, "Do you know those girls down there?"

Yakima glanced at her and chuckled. "What? Huh. Oh, them." He returned his gaze to the parlor house. "Can't tell for sure, but…"

"I take it you know the place," Annie said, pinching her lips together primly but also quirking her mouth corners into a smile.

"Oh, I reckon. A little." Yakima chuckled sheepishly.

"What kind of place is that?" Beth asked from where she sat on the chestnut behind Annie.

"You never mind," Annie told her.

"Oh," Beth said, nodding slowly and smiling around her sister at Yakima, "*that* kind of place."

"Men," Annie said, and rolled her eyes.

"Are we going down there, Yakima?" Beth asked.

Yakima glanced beyond the girls to see a big freight wagon lumbering to the hill's crest behind six stout, sweat-lathered mules and said above the wagon's growing din including the sharp cracks of the driver's bullwhip, "I'm going down but I want you two to stay up here and out of sight. I'm gonna perch you on that knoll up yonder." He pointed toward a pine-studded rise on the trail's far side, opposite the town.

"You mean you want us to wait *here* while you go down *there?*" Annie said, obviously nonplussed.

"That's right. Dangerous down there. Not a place for two nice girls. Don't worry—I won't be long," he said as the freight wagon lumbered past them, the burly, bearded driver giving both girls more than a passing glance. A cold cigar jutted from one side of his mouth.

The man looked at Annie and gave a loud rebel yell. "You should be workin' for Miss Petry, pretty girl!"

"See what I mean?" Yakima said.

Annie rolled her eyes at the uncouth driver. "I get your point." She gave Yakima a suspicious look, narrowing her eyes. "Just what will you be doing down there, if I may ask?"

Yakima glanced at the girls on the roof again, chuckled sheepishly, removed his hat and swept his hand through his long hair. "Nothin' like what you're thinkin'. We're low on supplies." He reached down to pat the canvas war bag hanging from his saddle horn. "Time to restock the larder for the final pull to Cannonball."

"What if something happens to you down there?" Annie asked, jerking her chin toward the gulch.

"It won't. Come on, girls."

Yakima reined Wolf off the trail and through the pines, climbing the slight grade toward the knoll. The girl's question played through his mind. She'd had a point. What if something did happen to him down there?

With him being who he was, there was always a good chance of something happening to him. Especially in a perdition like Deadwood Gulch.

When he halted the stallion at the base of the knoll, which was far enough off the trail that he didn't think the girls could be seen from the road, he swung down from his saddle and opened his left saddlebag pouch. He pulled out a lump cloth and removed the cloth to reveal a Merwin & Hulbert .31 pocket pistol.

He walked over to where Annie had stopped the chestnut and helped each girl down to the ground. He held the pistol up to Annie and asked, "Ever shot one of these before?"

"A gun? Yes."

"How good can you handle one?"

Annie hiked a shoulder. "Pa taught me to shoot a .44 Revolver sorta like your own as well as a Spencer repeating rifle. He knew he was going to die and he wanted me to be able to protect Beth and Ma." With saucy aplomb, she plucked the pistol from Yakima's hand, opened the loading gate and spun the cylinder.

"Not bad," Yakima said. "If you run into any trouble up here, use that to help you out of it. I'll hear the shot and come runnin'."

Beth looked up at the big man warily. "You will come back for us, won't you, Yakima?"

"Of course, I will, half-pint."

"I'm scared to be alone out here. I mean, since you started ridin' with us an' all. I don't want to go back to bein' alone."

"You won't." Yakima nudged her chin. "That's a

promise."

He grabbed his reins and swung up onto Wolf's back. "Stay put, now. Don't go near the trail. If all goes as planned, I should be back in a half-hour, forty-five minutes at the most."

"If you're not?" Annie asked, holding the pistol down low against her side.

"I will be."

Yakima clucked to Wolf and reined away. As he dropped back down through the pines, he told himself to be damn careful in town. He didn't have only himself to look out for anymore. He had two young girls to get to Cannonball. He'd also promised to get that letter and money belt to Paul's son. For the first time since Faith had died, he had other people depending on him.

He hadn't realized how much he'd liked the feeling.

It was a burden, as well. One that he vowed to carry through to the end.

Chapter 15

As Yakima rode down Deadwood's main street, he kept to the street's far right side. He rode with his chin down, hat brim pulled low over his eyes. He didn't want to be recognized.

He didn't even want to be in town, but he and the girls, both of whom ate almost as much as he did, had polished off the last of the small deer he'd shot just after leaving the White River, and they were out of several other staples, as well.

Including grain for the horses.

It was all right, he told himself. He knew Deadwood's layout well enough to get in and out quickly and efficiently. He'd ride in and out anonymously. He could do it. He'd done it before though being a six-foot-four-inch half-breed didn't make it easy.

Just then, a high-pitched, nasal female voice cut

through the din of the street around him with: "Yakima? *Yakima Henry?* That you?"

If wishes had wings, pigs would fly!

Yakima gritted his teeth. Keeping his head down, he continued riding.

"Hey, Yakima! Look up here, you old half-breed side-winder! It's Polly!"

Damn!

It looked like the only way he was going to get the cussed filly to shut up before his name spread all over town like a wildfire was to stop and exchange a few words with her. Drawing back on Wolf's reins, he turned the horse half-way around and gazed up at a blond young lady in her mid-to-late twenties leaning forward over the second-floor balcony rail of a little pink house with a red light in its front window.

"Uh...hello, there, Polly." Yakima feigned a smile then glanced around to see just how much attention the girl had called to him.

Too damn much for comfort, he quickly discovered. Nearly every person on the street had paused to peer in his direction, some taking longer looks than others.

"Haven't seen you through here in a while," Polly said, resting her arms atop the rail before her and setting her chin atop her hands.

She was pretty despite too much henna in her hair and

a missing front tooth, a little discoloration remaining from a black eye. She was still a young woman but aging quickly, as per the fine lines around her mouth and eyes, a certain weariness to her smile. Her features reminded Yakima a little of Annie. He fleetingly imagined Annie standing up there in such cheap and skimpy attire, looking coquettish but old before her time.

Sadness touched him. He was doubly glad of having gotten her away from Hat Creek Station.

"I've been in Arizona," Yakima said, wanting desperately to get off the street but not wanting to be rude to Polly, either. He took another quick glance around the street. Most folks were going about their business, but he didn't like the looks a couple of gun-hung men still scrutinizing him from the far side of the street, from the opposite side of a parked freight wagon.

Returning his gaze to the whore, he said, "Spent the last coupla years in the desert down there. Just got back north. Only came to town for some trail supplies." He patted the canvas warbag hanging from his saddlehorn. "Well, nice chatting with—"

"Gonna come see me later?" Polly asked with a smile and flirtatious bat of her eyes.

"I'd love to," Yakima said. "And I purely would but I'm just makin' a quick trip to town. I gotta get back on down the trail. Burnin' daylight, don't ya know!"

"Where you goin'?" the girl asked, keeping her chin on her crossed hands.

Yakima glanced toward the freight wagon again. The three men who'd been peering furtively at him from over the top of it were now turned to each other in what appeared serious discussion.

He reluctantly turned to the girl again and said, "Montana. Just passin' through." No point in announcing where he was really headed. He smiled broadly and pointed Wolf up the street, pinching his hat brim to the girl and saying, "I best be gettin' along. You take care of yourself now, Polly!"

"Hey, Yakima—what's the big hurry?" the girl yelled behind him, causing him to stretch his lips back from his teeth in frustration as he booted Wolf on ahead. He threw up a hand to her as a final good-bye and nudged Wolf into a trot.

As he weaved through the midday traffic, he glanced over his left shoulder. He couldn't see the three men now because of the horseback riders and wagons passing between him and them. He turned his head forward, hoping their interest in him had been only a passing one. Better yet, maybe they were ogling the half-dressed whore.

He didn't think so. Their eyes had been on him, all right.

As he weaved his way through the traffic, he debated aborting his mission here in Deadwood. He didn't figure he could do that. He planned to take the old Bismarck-Deadwood stagecoach trail north of here, and he didn't think there was any sizeable town within a two days' ride where he might be able to buy supplies. He himself could travel on game meat alone, but he wanted better for the girls. They needed potatoes, canned greens, salt, sugar, flour and syrup for pancakes.

He decided to go ahead and chance a short stop at a big mercantile owned by a friendly Irishman he remembered from previous trips, for another glance behind him revealed no shadowers. The interest that the three men had shown in him might have been more the workings of his overly cautious imagination than anything else.

At least, he hoped so.

He swung Wolf up to W.L. O'Shaughnessy's Mercantile and Feed Store—a sprawling, green frame building with a freshly painted red sign, complete with a green four-leaf clover painted at each end, stretched across its peaked third story. A spotted white dog lounged on its side in the shade beneath the awning stretching halfway over the broad loading dock. The dog lifted its head a little and worked its flat nose as Yakima pulled Wolf up to one of the several hitchracks. The dog thumped its tail a couple of times in friendly greeting then lay its head back down and returned to sleep.

It was another warm Indian summer day—a good

day to sack out in the shade. Yakima wished he could do likewise.

He swung down from Wolf's back, grabbed the warbag from his saddle and loosely tied the horse's reins to the hitchrack then mounted the porch and pushed inside through the heavy wooden door boasting a curtained glass pane and an OPEN sign in its upper panel. The main counter ran across the wall to the right, beyond where two men dressed in the cheap, gaudy suits of traveling drummers, played cards at one of the four small tables arranged in the open area between the door and the counter, near a cold potbelly stove.

A big man in a green apron, nearly bald except for some stringy colorless hair slithering straight back across his scalp, and wearing a colorless mustache and goatee, stood behind the bar, smoking a pipe and staring toward the drummers whom he'd been conversing with until he'd heard the door over the bell ring. Now he turned toward Yakima, as did the drummers.

Yakima didn't usually warrant passing glances. Today was no exception. Of course, men of every stripe milled about the streets of Deadwood—soldiers, buffalo hunters, Indians, half-breeds, blacks, Chinese and husky bearded men speaking in northern European accents. Still, Yakima's size alone as well as the jade eyes set in deep sockets in his handsomely if severely chiseled, copper face nearly always warranted close study. The low-crowned black hat, the buckskins and the pistol on one hip, bowie knife on the other, added even more interest.

Frontiersman?

Gunslinger?

Outlaw?

Neither the big man behind the counter nor the drummers said anything. They stared, eyes wide with interest. Yakima didn't mind. He was used to it.

He didn't mind as long as no one recognized him as a wanted man and decided to call the authorities or try to earn the bounty themselves.

"Afternoon," Yakima said, pinching his hat brim to the big man behind the counter. He glanced around. "Where's O'Shaughnessy?"

The big man knocked his pipe dottle into an ash tray on the counter before him, beside a couple of folded newspapers. He took a drag and said tightly, "Dead."

"What happened?"

The big man tapped his chest. "Ticker."

Yakima frowned, curious. "How come…?"

He didn't have to finish the question. The big man must have heard the query a lot. "I kept the name because mine is Schitz. Pfieffer Schitz." He glowered at Yakima, drawing his mouth corners down.

The drummers, who'd returned to their card game,

chuckled.

Yakima gave a wry chuff. "I see your point." He cast a cautious glance through the door's window. Relieved to not see anyone who looked like trouble lurking out on the street nearby, he strode to the counter and plopped the warbag on top of it. "I need this filled. Usual stuff along with some cheese, sausage, and crackers. A few pickles, too. Throw in some chocolate and some candy—a nickel's worth of each." He hesitated, pondering, then said, "And a couple of pretty hair ribbons."

Pfieffer Schitz gave him an arch-browed skeptical look, shrugged, then moseyed off to fill the order.

"Oh, and five pounds of oats," Yakima called to the man's broad back.

Schitz threw up an acknowledging hand.

While he was gone, roaming around the cluttered store that smelled like everything from smoked meat and cheese to gunpowder and meal, Yakima kept an eye on the window to his right, glad to still see no trouble stirring out on the street. Just the usual mix of the Deadwood crowd passing by the store or clustered in front of the Nightingale Saloon on the street's opposite side.

When Schitz had lined up all the goods on the counter and tallied up the cost on a notepad with a pencil, Yakima paid the man the eight-dollars and sixty-six cents, wincing at the regrettable lightening of his grubstake. He wanted Beth to have the candy, though. And he wanted Annie to have some ribbons to pin in her hair when she met up with her grandparents again. That would make both girls feel good and they hadn't had anything to feel good about in a long time.

He shoved the grub, candy and hair ribbons into his war bag until it grew so fat he had trouble closing it, then slung the strap over his shoulder. He grabbed the five pounds of oats, bid the mercantiler good day, then turned and strode to the door.

He stopped in front of it, peering out, and froze.

Ah, shit.

Four men stood facing him in the middle of the street, which had quieted down considerably. In fact, it was practically deserted. At least, it was in front of the mercantile. No wagons or horseback riders passed from either direction.

Yakima now saw that a fifth man stood behind the other four, flanking them on their left. He had his hand on the butt of his holstered .45 but had not yet drawn the weapon. The other four had all drawn their pistols and were holding them straight down along their legs.

The four, all dressed in three-piece suits and broad-brimmed Stetsons, were giving Yakima hard-eyed stares.

The fifth man, a gray-haired, gray-eyed man, Yakima recognized as a man called The Reverend. The Reverend had acquired the nickname due to his penchant for dressing all in black—back shirt, black ribbon tie, black pants, black boots and black hat. He was smiling like the cat that ate the canary, but his eyes were cold and flat beneath the broad brim of his black hat.

He was a bounty killer. A notorious one.

Jack DeLong was his real name. Delong was an older man, late-fifties. He led up the four others, whose names Yakima did not know. All he knew was that the Reverend led up the bunch of kill-hungry bounty hunters who called themselves the Angels of Death because they went after only men with "dead or alive" bounties on their heads, because they always brought their quarries in toe down and ready for the old wooden overcoat.

"Ah, shit," Yakima said again...

Just before he opened the door and stepped outside.

Chapter 16

Yakima moved slowly out onto the loading dock.

He came to a stop at the edge of it and let the feed sack roll off his right shoulder, freeing up that hand for his gun.

All four men before him, keeping their expressions stony, slowly raised their revolvers, pointing the barrels at Yakima.

Yakima looked at the black-clad, gray-mustached Reverend and said, "What is this, Preacher—an execution?"

The Reverend blinked slowly then slid his gaze to the four men holding their guns on Yakima. His shrewd smile remaining on his lips, he said, "Give him a chance, boys. Against the law to kill a man…less'n he draws first."

He glanced to his right and left, where crowds of on-lookers had gathered on the boardwalks on both sides of the street, a cautious fifty feet away. Men as well as women comprised the crowd. A few boys and dogs. Even a little ginger-haired girl in pigtails with a straw hat. They all stared, riveted on the proceedings, quiet as church mice.

The Reverend's four gun-wolves glanced at the Reverend then turned their heads back to Yakima. Slowly, a little reluctantly, Yakima thought, all four holstered their revolvers but kept their hands on their pistol butts.

"You might get one, even two," the Reverend told Yakima. "But not all four."

If the four gun-wolves had any reaction to that, none betrayed it. Well, one did. The tallest of the four, who wore a thick dragoon-style mustache over his thin-lipped mouth. A blue vein throbbed on the left side of his forehead. Just beneath it, a sweat bead popped up, glistening in the sunshine and ran down toward his left brow.

"I'm gonna count to five," the Reverend called across the nearly silent street.

He removed his own hand from the grips of his holstered Colt, apparently confident he wouldn't need it.

"One," he called. "Two...three...four..."

Before he could get out the "five," a girl's shrill voice caromed over the street: "You got him outnumbered, you cowardly devils!"

The screeching, ever-so-vaguely familiar voice was followed by two quick gunshots.

That made everyone on the street, including Yakima

and the four wolves and the Reverend facing him, nearly jump out of their boots. As the two bullets kicked up dirt a few feet shy of the gun wolves, having come from Yakima's left, the four bounty hunters slapped leather, drew iron and wheeled to confront the unexpected threat.

As they did, Yakima jerked his own .44 from its holster and, crouching, went to work on the gun wolves just as, realizing they'd been whipsawed, turned back toward him, eyes snapping wide in horror. They swung their guns toward him, aiming, but only one got off a shot before Yakima's bullets chewed through each man in turn, jerked them back into bizarre little screaming death dances before their knees buckled and they piled up in the ground dirt and horse dung.

Still crouching, legs bent at the knees, Yakima swung the Colt toward the Reverend and fired. His bullet tore into the corner of the building the man had been standing in front of just as the black-clad bounty hunter wheeled and ran around that corner and out of sight.

"Mount up, Yakima!" Annie screamed to Yakima's left.

He turned to see the two girls gallop the chestnut out from a break between a bank and a hardware store. They swung the horse toward Yakima and hooves drummed loudly in the heavy silence after the gunfire as the pair galloped toward him, the chestnut's head down, ears laid back, Annie gazing wild-eyed toward Yakima, her blond hair blowing back behind her in the wind.

Beth was snugged up tight to her sister's back, peering around Annie's left side.

The crowd stared in shocked silence at the dead men on the street, at Yakima and the two girls—one barely knee-high to a grasshopper!—galloping toward the big half-breed. Yakima was befuddled as everyone else on the street, but he was not befuddled enough to look a gift horse in the mouth. He had no idea what the girls were doing in town, but now that they were here and had more or less saved his hide he wasn't going to bother just yet with fool questions.

A low roar was rising from the onlookers, the men and women and children looking around at each other and muttering in shocked surprise.

Yakima holstered his Colt, grabbed the feed sack and the warbag, leaped from the boardwalk to the street. When he had the feed and grubsack tied to his saddle, he ripped the reins from the hitchrack and swung up onto Wolf's back. The girls and the chestnut approached, Annie drawing back on her horse's reins.

"Don't slow down—keep goin', honey!" Yakima yelled, then booted Wolf west along the street, the direction from which they'd come. Annie did the same to the chestnut and side by side, Annie and Beth and the chestnut and Yakima and Wolf high-tailed it.

After a block's hard ride through the gaping, milling onlookers, some pointing them out to others, Yakima yelled to Annie, "Take a right!"

He turned Wolf down the side street and Annie, directly behind him now, turned the chestnut.

Soon they put the town behind them. Yakima turned them onto the old Bismarck-Deadwood stage road. He kept Wolf galloping for a good half-mile before he drew rein on the shoulder of a low hill and held up his right hand for Annie to do likewise.

He stared in mute exasperation at the two dust and sweat-streaked girls sitting the blowing chestnut beside him. Annie's face blossomed into a proud smile. "Saw you needed a little help back there!"

Yakima gave a caustic chuff. "I don't know whether to hug you and kiss you or to bend you over my knee." He shook his head in bewilderment as he looked back toward town, glad to not see any pursuers. Turning back to Annie and Beth, he said, "I told you two to stay on that hill!"

"If we had," Beth said with customary haughtiness, "you'd be pushing up daisies, Yakima Henry!"

Annie said, "I got worried when I saw those five men head toward the mercantile we saw you go into and then the street clearing so fast afterwards. I could tell trouble was brewing."

Of course, from their high vantage point, the girls had

been able to keep an eye on him as he'd moved through the town. He looked at the Merwin & Hulbert shoved down behind Annie's belt. "You two could have been killed. Damn lucky you weren't. But," he added with a weary shake of his head, "since we're all three still upright, I reckon I can save that hide-tannin' for later."

"Thank you," Annie said.

He frowned at her. "Did you fire those shots?"

Annie slid the revolver up from behind her belt and blew on the end of the barrel. "Not bad, eh?"

"Not bad if you tried to miss."

Annie pursed her lips and shook her head. "Oh, I couldn't shoot them in the back. Pa taught me that shooting a man in the back was about the lowdown dirtiest thing you can do to even your worst enemy. Even if they had you outnumbered. Besides, from seein' you shoot before, I knew all I needed to do was distract them for a second, even up the odds and you'd get the drop. And I was right."

Annie turned her head to one side and winked.

"All right," Yakima said with a dry chuckle, pointing Wolf up the trail that curved ahead around the side of a sloping, pine-studded mountain. "Let's put some distance between us and Deadwood. The leader of that bunch got away, but I have a hunch we haven't seen the last of him."

***

They followed the old stage road north and west through-out the warm afternoon, trekking through breathtakingly beautiful country of slab-sided mesas and low mountains carpeted in the blue green of spruces and firs. The foliage along the several creeks they crossed was the deep reds and golden browns of autumn. Most of the aspens shone white-stemmed amongst the conifers, for this far north they had by now lost their leaves.

Seeing that made Yakima shiver. He had another two-week ride to Fort Abercrombie from here by way of Cannonball. He'd be turning around and riding back in November. The nights as well as the days got cold in November. Arizona had thinned his blood. He was liable to freeze to his saddle.

Why in hell had he ever left Arizona, anyway? Probably a damn fool move. But, then, he'd left a lot of trouble down there centered around an old Spanish church and its cache of Jesuit gold. Gold that had been mined by the Jesuits' Apache slaves. The slaves had placed a curse on the church.

Now, Yakima had not earlier been the suspicious sort. He hadn't believed in such huck as curses.

He did now.

Anywhere there was gold, let alone *cursed* gold, there

was trouble. Just like anywhere there were pretty women, there was trouble, as well. Between the gold and the women, Yakima had been hip deep in it. When he'd gotten it all resolved, it had been time to move on.

He was and always had been a moving-on kind of fella.

"Was she pretty?"

Annie's voice had plucked him out of his reverie. He glanced at her, realizing he'd been staring off with a fritter-eating grin on his mug.

Neck warming, he grinned and said, "Both of 'em."

"There were two of them?" Annie asked, incredulous. She and Beth rode beside him on the long-untended trail scored with ruts and brush and pocked by chuckholes.

"You get around some—don't ya, Yakima?" Beth said with a sly grin.

"Oh, look there—a sign in the brush," he said, glad to have a reason to change the subject.

He rode over to the trail's right side and look down at where a sign lay partly against the rotted, three-foot-high post it had rotted off of. The faded painting announced: MOUSE CREEK STATION. A miniature, painted hand at the bottom pointed up at a slant toward the sign's top right corner.

Yakima looked ahead to see where a secondary trail branched off from the main one, to the right and angling up and over a low hill at the top of which a large oak stood spidery and nearly leafless, its soft yellow leaves lying like gold drops at the base of its broad trunk.

Yakima glanced at the sun angling low in the west, pushing broad, purple shadows relieved by the sun's own deep reds and salmons glistening on cedars and pines and silhouetting several low western ridges against it.

"What is it, Yakima?" Beth asked.

"We might have found a place to hole up for the night—inside for a change. Follow me, ladies. Let's check it out." As he nudged Wolf into a trot ahead, he glanced over his shoulder and narrowed one eye. "Stay behind me. Someone else might have had the same idea."

He turned Wolf off the main trail and onto the secondary one. With Annie and Beth trailing fifty feet behind, he rode up and over the hill. The trail continued for maybe a quarter mile where it curved around in front of a squat log cabin sporting a good half-dozen cougar pelts stretched from steel spikes on its front and near sides. Cougar hides appeared to be the cabin's windows, as well.

"Hello, the cabin!" Yakima called as he reined Wolf up in front of the humble place.

The only response was the sifting of the wind through the surrounding spruces and firs.

Yakima looked around. No one was about. But the chimney pipe didn't have a lid on it, which usually meant it had been employed recently. Also, a stack of recently split wood abutted the cabin's front wall, to the right of the door, which appeared not to be latched.

A small, roofed stoop fronted the door. There was corrugated tin washtub on it, on a log rail pedestal. The unpainted pine boards that had been used to build the porch were relatively new. Newer than the cabin, anyway, which had likely been built back in the late-70s, when the stage line had started business and had built a string of relay and overnight stations along its route.

Yakima called out again. Again receiving no response, he stepped out of his saddle and dropped his reins.

He glanced at the girls who had stopped twenty feet behind him and were eyeing him warily.

"Stay here."

As he started toward the stoop, he flicked the keeper thong free of his gun hammer but left the .44 in its holster. He stepped up onto the stoop, moving slowly and quietly, then gently nudged open the unlatched door. It creaked inward on dry leather hinges. When he'd pushed it half-way open, the light pushing into the cabin from behind him glinted off an octagonal rifle barrel aimed at his heart. The light slid up the rifle's stock to reveal the two thick, age-gnarled hands holding it.

The man the hands belonged to stepped forward out of the shadows and pressed the barrel against Yakima's chest. Not hard but not a love tap, neither.

"What do you want?" the old man croaked.

He was maybe seventy with a fleshy, bearded face, liver spots dotting his forehead, which was pale above the red line of a deep, leathery weathering. His head was nearly bald though his ears were tufted with hair resembling small balls of steel wool. His large bloodshot eyes were tobacco brown.

Yakima raised his hands half-high. "Was just wonderin' if the place was occupied."

With the end of the gun barrel, the old man pushed Yakima two steps back onto the stoop and glanced at the girls sitting the chestnut behind the black, who eyed the old man warily. "Who're they?"

"Two girls just wonderin' if the place was occupied," Yakima told him, keeping his hands raised.

The old man smiled shrewdly. "Was thinkin' about spendin' the night, was you?"

"We were thinkin' about it."

"The little one over there—she looks meaner'n a stick-teased diamondback."

Yakima glanced at Beth. "You got that right."

"What do you say we boil her up for supper? I haven't had me little-girl stew in a coon's age!"

Yakima cut his eyes at Beth again. She was scowling her offence at the question. Annie sat astride the chestnut with her mouth halfway open in shock, but then a smile tugged at her mouth corners.

Returning his gaze to the old man, Yakima said, "I don't know—she might be a little tough and bony for stew."

"HAH!" the old man roared suddenly, lowering the Springfield rifle and extending his right hand to Yakima. "I was just joshin' about the little-girl stew. Hello, there, big feller. I'm Wildcat Jack!"

Yakima shook the old man's hand, the palm of which was crusted with hard callouses, no doubt from scraping wildcat hides. "Yakima Henry."

"And who're the pretty ladies?"

"The oldest one there is Annie. Beth's the diamond-back."

"I was just joshin' ya about lookin' mean, honey. Why, you're cuter'n a speckled pup. Why, soon you'll be rivaling your sister in the looks department!

Despite the compliment he'd paid her, Beth kept regarding the man suspiciously. Annie flushed and lowered her eyes demurely.

Wildcat Jack turned to Yakima, smiling, showing a relatively full set of scraggly, tobacco-rimed teeth. "I been callin' this here old relay station home since the stage line folded five years ago. Nothin' official. I just moved in an' hunt mountain lions for area ranchers. I sell the hides in Deadwood. You're welcome to spend the night and share my grub an' my fire an' the whole durn ball of wax!"

He smiled more broadly, glancing at the girls. "I don't get many visitors, an' I sure do get tired of talkin' to my mules. Go ahead and stable your hosses with old Fred an' Bunnie. There's a barn and stable back in the trees behind the cabin. Then come on back an' wash up and I'll cook you a stew you won't never forget!"

Wildcat Jack looked at Beth. "Guess what's in it?"

Beth glanced at the wildcat hides stretched out and nearly covering every square inch of the cabin's outside walls. Turning back to the bearded old man, she said with a distasteful air, "Wildcat?"

"Darn tootin'!" Jack said with a roaring laugh.

Chapter 17

Wildcat Jack turned out to be a grand host.

And while not a large man physically, he turned out to be a larger-than-life figure with a big personality teeming with ribald jokes and hearty laughter. He took to the girls right away, showing them card tricks and pulling coins out of their ears.

While he whipped up his wildcat stew from a fresh haunch, his pet crow, Henry, flew in and out of the cabin's open door, taking Wildcat Jack's offerings of scrap meat and fat he cut from the haunch. It was apparently such a time-worn tradition that Jack didn't even look up as the bird flew in and perched on his shoulder and cawed, rolling his ink-black eyes down toward the fresh meat on the cutting board.

Continuing to chop with his other hand and talking and laughing raucously non-stop, leaping from topic to topic so fast it was difficult for Yakima to follow, Jack plucked another morsel of meat from his cutting board and gave it to Henry before Henry flew back out the door to enjoy the food from the privacy of the porch rail.

The girls and even Yakima were fascinated by this. Beth, who was slow to warm up to anybody, was quick to warm up to Wildcat Jack. Not long after she'd washed up on the porch and stepped into the cabin, Jack had her cackling with free and easy laughter. She followed him around closely, watching with great interest everything he did while Annie drifted around the cabin, scrutinizing all the game trophies and animal skins and hides tacked to the cabin walls and hanging from ceiling beams as well as the vast array of hunting and trapping paraphernalia.

An ambrotype photo in a scrolled gold case sat on a shelf between the sleeping area of the cabin and the small parlor. Annie inspected this especially closely. It was a wedding photograph—a man in a suit sitting in some photographer's studio parlor while a woman stood beside him in a flowing white wedding dress and holding a bouquet of flowers to her bosom. While many years younger, the man was obviously Jack—almost clean-shaven, wearing only a neatly trimmed mustache. His hair was combed to one side, showing comb tracks in the pomade.

The woman was strikingly beautiful—a tall, cameo-pretty brunette with hair piled atop her head in thick coils with ringlets hanging over her forehead and sausage curls dangling down in front of her ears.

The stew was thick and rich and meaty. Jack had cooked the chopped haunch to perfection, charring it lightly in a skillet before dumping it into the stew pot in which he'd already added potatoes, carrots, turnips and onions from the garden he irrigated behind the old station barn, which housed a milk cow and several chickens, Yakima had noted while he and the girls had tended their horses.

The girls didn't appear to enjoy the stew quite as much as Yakima did. He'd supped on wildcat meat before and found it, while a little tough and gamey, a nice change from his usual beef, sowbelly and wild game. To him it tasted a little like grouse or sage hen.

The girls might have taken each spoonful of the stew timidly, but there was nothing timid about their wide-eyed and laughing appreciation of Jack's running, raucous conversation as he related his many run-ins with Indians and bears over the years as well as his former career as a bank robber with none other than the Ben Carson and Joe Wallace Bunch from down in Missouri—rivals of Jesse James and Cole Younger, whom Jack claimed he'd beat at cards once in Abilene, Kansas. Drunk, Cole threatened to cut out his heart until Jack nudged him with the sawed-off shotgun he was aiming at Cole's belly from under the table.

Jack claimed Cole turned white as a sheet and broke out in a sweat.

Jack slapped the table and laughed.

Out on the porch rail, Henry cawed as though with his own appreciation of the tale.

While the girls washed the dishes and put them away, Jack and Yakima played two-handed poker. Jack was one of those men who seemed infinitely more interested in himself and what he had to say than he was in his guest. He'd been curious about where Yakima and the girls were headed and why, but after Yakima had filled him in, his curiosity about his guests seemed to have been satisfied. He just continued telling jokes and talking about his own exploits.

Yakima didn't mind it a bit. In fact, he welcomed it. If there was one topic that bored him to tears, that topic was himself. He was far more interested in other people. Jack was one interesting fellow.

Around ten o'clock, Jack took an old fiddle down off the wall, blew the dust off it, and started to play. Yakima and the girls sat at the kitchen table, Yakima sipping Jack's homemade chokecherry wine, the girls each savoring tall glasses of rich, creamy cow's milk, enjoying the music. Jack proved to be an uncommonly good fiddler especially after he'd warmed up with a couple of old mournful Irish ballads. When he sawed into "Sweet Betsy from Pike," he gained his stride.

Soon, Annie and Beth were dancing together on the hemp-braided parlor rug. Yakima didn't consider himself much of a dancer, but when the girls pulled him out of his chair, he managed a few do-si-does, hooking arms and turning each girl in circles on the rug, clapping his hands and stomping his feet to the rhythms of Jack's buoyant fiddling.

After a half hour or so, Yakima donned his hat and left the cabin, sweating, needing air.

Also, he wanted to take a close look around the cabin before rolling into his blankets. He'd been careful to watch his and the girls' backtrail, in case anyone had shadowed them out from Deadwood. He was pretty sure no one had. Still, he had to make sure no one was on the lurk, maybe waiting for the lamps to be snuffed before making his or their move for the bounty on his head.

Taking deep breaths of the cool, clean Dakota air spiced with the tang of pine and sage, he stepped off the stoop and traced several slow, broad circles around the cabin and inspected the barn and corral. He noted that Wolf and the chestnut as well as Jack's mules all seemed settled peacefully in for the night, which was a good sign that all was quiet out here. The animals would know if there was trouble.

Satisfied, Yakima walked out to where Mouse Creek

chuckled through the pines just south of Jack's cabin.

He stood on the bank of the creek, watching and listening.

When he detected no unnatural sounds, he found himself remaining, enjoying the dark-stemmed trees and the glinting water rippling over rocks as well as the stars flour-dusted across the vast firmament between the black bastions of two mountains widely set apart, one to his right, one to his left. He untied his moccasins, kicked out of them, and removed his socks. He stepped into the stream, bathing his feet.

More than bathing them.

Being in the company of young girls must have taught him the joy of simple pleasures.

He smiled at the thought. "I'll be damned," he told himself as he stepped into the cold stream, feeling the rocks and pebbles bite against the undersides of his feet. "Imagine forgetting something like that."

Footsteps sounded behind him. There was nothing furtive about them, so he did not overreact. Something had told him she'd come. She'd probably been watching him from the cabin, charting his course around it and the barn and then down to the creek.

He glanced over his shoulder to see her slender figure take shape in the darkness. She stopped at the edge of the trees. She wore a blanket around her shoulders. Her hair, freshly brushed, flowed across her shoulders, glistening in the moonlight.

She said nothing. She just stared at him from the bank.

She sat on a log to remove her shoes and socks. Holding her skirt up to her knees, she stepped slowly off the bank and into the stream. She walked up beside him, looked up at him, the star- and moonlight shimmering in her wide, dark eyes. Her lips were slightly parted. He could see the edges of her teeth.

Her expression was sober, thoughtful, wistful.

She smiled.

She took his hand in hers and they stood together in the stream, the water feeling cold and pure and refreshing as it slid over their feet and lapped up against their ankles. They stood there together, holding hands, staring at the sky through the silhouetted pine boughs, at the shimmering stars and the silently rising moon.

He could feel her pulse against his palm.

She could feel his.

***

"Thanks for the hospitality, Jack," Yakima said the next day as they all stood together in the yard with the saddled horses. He shook Jack's hand.

"Thanks for stopping by!" Jack said, pumping Yakima's hand with his own firm grip. "I truly do appreciate it. A fella gets lonely this far out in the high an' rocky." He glanced at the girls standing by the chestnut whose reins Annie was holding. "An' there's a darn paucity of purty faces, too!"

He smiled broadly and walked over and tussled Beth's hair. "Goodbye, little muskrat. You got a kiss for Jack?"

"Why not?" Beth said.

Jack bent down and Beth planted a kiss on the old man's bearded cheek. He straightened, touching the spot where the girl had kissed him. "I ain't gonna wash that cheek for a good, long time." He glanced at Yakima standing behind him. "Not that I ever do, anyway!"

He laughed and turned to Annie.

"Good-bye, honey. You take care, now hear?"

He moved in for a hug and Annie stepped forward to oblige him, hugging him tightly. "You two, Wildcat Jack. Thanks for the vittles. They were delicious."

"Were they?" He sounded surprised.

"They sure were." Annie said with a little too much vigor. She elbowed her sister. "Weren't they Beth?"

"Oh," Beth said, caught off-guard. Her mouth a little stiff, she said, "Yessir—right tasty!"

Jack glanced at Yakima, winked and laughed.

Yakima helped the girls onto the chestnut's back then mounted Wolf, saying, "Take care, Jack. Say, can I offer you a couple of coins for…?"

"You do that," Jack snapped, his face swelling and flushing, "and you'll insult this old buzzard right to my rotten core!"

"All right, then," Yakima said, glancing at the girls then reining Wolf around.

"All right, then," Jack said. "Farewell!"

"Farewell, Wildcat Jack," Beth and Annie said.

And then they rode up and over the hill, leaving the lonely old wildcat hunter gazing after them, likely smiling with fond remembrance of the night they'd shared.

Yakima and the girls rode out to the main trail then continued north, feeling a little bad about leaving the old man alone again, probably feeling even lonelier than before they'd arrived. Preoccupied, Yakima was not aware of the Reverend standing just beneath the lip of a near hill, gazing at him and the girls through a spy glass.

Chapter 18

Late that afternoon, Yakima and the girls followed the badly rutted and overgrown trail to the crest of a hill. Yakima was about to start down the hill's other side but reined up suddenly, gazing down the hill and into the bowl of prairie spread out below him, saying, "Whoa!"

Annie checked down the chestnut beside him. She and Beth glanced at him curiously. "What is it?" Annie asked.

"Never seen that before."

"What?"

"That hotel down yonder."

Annie followed Yakima's gaze to the wood-frame, three-story building standing off the trail's right side. Yakima thought it looked relatively new, which it must have been, since he hadn't seen the place the last time he'd ridden through here maybe five years ago. That was around the same time the stage line had switched its route from Deadwood to Pierre, which had recently become a railroad hub, bypassing most of the old southern route.

A new trail had been carved off the main one. It ran southeast of the old one, rising and falling over the dun hills. That would be the dogleg added when the stage line switched its route through Fort Pierre. At the intersection of these two trails, the old and the new, the hotel sat on a large, hard-packed lot with what appeared a stable and two corrals.

Yakima studied the large painted sign stretched across the hotel's second story: JOHN THUNDER'S DOGLEG HOTEL.

"I'll be hanged," Yakima said. "I know John Thunder. Leastways, if it's the same John Thunder I once scouted Apaches with in the cavalry a few years back." It had been more than a few years back, but he was getting to the age when, on purpose or not, men started to underestimate the swiftness of time's passage.

He looked around the place. He didn't see anyone in the yard. No horses, either. The building didn't appear abandoned, however.

"Hmmm," he said. "Might be nice to sleep with a roof under our heads again tonight—wouldn't it darlin's?"

"You don't need to buy a hotel room for us, Yakima," Annie said. "We've been burden enough. You're gonna need your grubstake for the winter."

"Hey," Beth said, swatting her sister's arm, "speak for yourself!"

Yakima winked at the little girl, then said, "I'm speakin' for me. The older a man gets, the harder and colder the ground feels. We'll ride down an' see if the man who runs the place is the John Thunder I remember and how much he charges for his rooms." He was actually thinking of the girls more than himself. They'd spent enough nights on the hard ground and while the night before they'd slept with a roof over their heads, Yakima and the girls had slept on the floor. Wildcat Jack had offered his cot, but neither the girls nor Yakima would take the old man's comfortable bed and make him sleep on the floor.

"If you say so," Annie said with a shrug.

"He says so!" Beth said and gave her sister another swat.

"Ouch—cut it out, brat!"

"You cut it out!"

"I didn't—oh, never mind!" Annie said, gritting her teeth.

Chuckling, Yakima booted Wolf on down the hill.

He and the girls bottomed out and swerved off the trail just beyond where it intersected with the new dogleg and rode into the yard. Dust rose from their horses' hooves and wafted in the warm afternoon breeze.

Yakima studied the ground, finding the prints of many

shod hooves overlaying each other. Recent ones, too. Horse apples and mule fritters, as well.

Apparently, the place was still in business. The marks in the yard and the building's overall well-kept appearance told him that. It was nothing to write home about—just a three-story, frame, unpainted affair, albeit a sturdy-looking one, with a broad front porch on which several ladderback and wicker chairs sat. Several washtubs hung from nails in the front wall.

The front door was propped open with one of the chairs.

Yakima and the girls reined up at one of the two hitchracks, and Yakima swung down from the saddle. He looped his reins over the rack and glanced at the girls. "Wait here. I'll check it out."

"I'm hungry," Beth complained.

"Stop!" Annie scolded her.

"With any luck, you'll be dinin' soon, darlin'," Yakima said.

He walked up the porch steps and onto the porch, as usual releasing the keeper thong from over his Colt's hammer. He stopped just outside the propped-open door and gazed into the shadows, seeing only a fairly large, wooden-floored room stretching off before him to a set of stairs angling up the rear wall. There were maybe a dozen tables arranged neatly between Yakima and the stairs.

Flies buzzed against the several sunlit windows in the room's wall ahead and to Yakima's right. That and the faint creaking of the building were the only sounds issuing from the place.

"Hello?" Yakima called. "Anybody here?"

His voice echoed around the empty room before him. That was the only response he received.

Yakima stepped over the threshold and into what must be the place's dining room/saloon. He stopped just inside. A varnished oak bar ran along the wall to his left. It had a mirrored back bar, the head of an albino pronghorn mounted above the mirror. The mirror had been recently polished. It reflected the big half-breed clearly. Not a smudge on it, in fact. The bar had been recently polished, as well, and the same with the tables. The floor was well swept. No dust anywhere.

The place was in business, all right.

But where were the employees?

Yakima called, "John? John Thunder?"

Yakima walked across the room, his boots booming on the wooden floor. He glanced up the stairs and called, "John Thunder?" Again, only the echo of his own voice was returned to him.

He looked at the bar. Two doors flanked it, one near the front of the room, one near the back. He walked around behind the bar, opened the door, and poked his head through it. A well-appointed kitchen lay before him. The kitchen was warm and humid from two kettles simmering on the range against the wall to his left, near the other door leading out to the bar.

Yakima walked through the kitchen and used a scrap of cowhide lying on the counter to lift the lid off one pot. The aroma of beans and what he deemed was likely antelope wafted into his face, making his stomach groan with hunger. He lifted the lid from the other pot. That one was beans and beef. Both stews had plenty of onions and potatoes and were well-seasoned, to boot.

Damn! Even with all the provisions he'd purchased in Deadwood, he could go for a well-cooked stew.

Yakima returned the lid to the stew pot then walked over to the near door that let out behind the bar, passing in front of a curtained pantry as he did. He stepped out into the bar area and grunted with great surprise when two, large, brawny arms entangled themselves around his waist from behind, squeezing the air out of him and drawing him back against the big, fleshy, sour-smelling body flanking him and lifted him clear off his feet.

The man roared in his right ear, "Yakima Henry, you big ugly half-breed sinner—I can't believe you're still kickin'!"

The big man—even bigger than Yakima—set Yakima back down and backed away, laughing. Yakima swung around and rammed his fist toward the bigger man's bulging belly but did not connect. Scowling his confusion at the bigger man, he said, "How'd you sneak up on me like that? You're big as a Brahma bull, you old scudder!"

John Thunder threw his head back, laughing. He had long, shaggy, grizzled hair well speckled with gray and a beard of the same texture. The beard came a good half-way down his broad chest; a long, solid gray streak ran slantwise through it, resembling a lightning bolt.

Thunder was half-Sioux and he'd been a good tracker and packer in his day, despite his size. Because of that considerable size—six-foot-six and nearly three-hundred pounds—he always rode a stout Missouri mule.

He was dressed in a blue cotton work shirt, its tails hanging out of his baggy canvas trousers. He wore suspenders and a necktie that did not go with the shirt but which he apparently thought made him appear more respectable, since obviously it was a respectable place here he was trying to run. Also hanging around his neck was what appeared the same ancient tobacco sack he'd worn around his neck back when he and Yakima were stationed together at Fort Hildebrandt in Arizona. Fort Hell, everyone had called the encampment and it had been aptly dubbed. Apaches had been a constant threat; in fact, once they'd even sacked the fort.

Thunder had made the tobacco pouch himself from

a bull's scrotum.

"Ah, hell, you're still sore after all these years that I can still move quieter than you can?" Thunder slapped his knee and laughed.

Again, Yakima scowled, puzzled. "What're you doin' down here, John? I thought you was sutler at Fort Lincoln."

"I was, but then I heard they carved a dogleg off the old stage trail. I heard it was gonna be a boomin' business, with cattle herds passin' through on the way to Pierre. I'd saved up a stake, so I moved down here and built this place damn near all myself—just two other fellas helpin'." He slapped Yakima's shoulder and guffawed. "Been a gold mine! I've only been here two years and it's already almost paid for itself!"

Yakima glanced back into the main room then frowned again at his large friend. "Where's all your customers, ya braggart?"

"It's quiet durin' the day, but things pick up at night when the freight trains start rollin' through." Thunder grinned, showing one silver front tooth. He rolled his eyes toward the ceiling. "Got me a couple of girls upstairs. Brought 'em from the hogpen at Fort Mandan. Cute as speckled pups!"

"As much of a blowhard as ever, but I'll be damned if it ain't good seein' you again, John!" Yakima said, laughing and reaching up to pinch the big man's fat, weathered cheeks above his beard. "How much will you sell me a couple of rooms for, you old scudder?"

Thunder frowned skeptically. "*Rooms?* You got someone with ya? Yakima, you *never* got no one with ya."

Yakima jerked his chin toward the door then walked toward it. Thunder followed, his own deerskin moccasins making rasping sounds across the wooden floor. He followed Yakima out onto the stoop then stood beside him.

Yakima glanced at the two girls who had dismounted the chestnut and stood beside it, Annie holding the reins. Yakima said, "John Thunder, I'd like you to meet my two purty traveling companions—Miss Annie Drake and her little sis, Beth."

Thunder glanced at Yakima, humor in his eyes. "They just keep gettin' younger and younger!" He turned to the girls and hooded his eyes. "An' purtier'n purtier."

Annie blushed. Beth stared at the big roguish halfbreed with her head tilted a little to one side, the usual skeptical expression on her face.

Thunder turned to Yakima. "I tell you what—since you're packin' beauty this time around, I'll give you two rooms, three bowls of stew and my own bread fresh out'n the oven in one hour…free of charge…if you chop me a stack of wood and tip a few back at the bar with me later."

Yakima smiled. "You sure? I got jingle."

"Keep your grubstake. You're gonna need it this winter. Besides, I still owe you for a poker game you staked me to back in Tucson."

"You got it, pard. Wood around back?"

"Yep."

Yakima patted the man's shoulder. "I'll get started as soon as I've tended our hosses."

Thunder turned to the girls. "In the meantime, why don't you two help me heat water so you each can have a long hot bath?"

Even Beth smiled at the proposal.

Chapter 19

Yakima spent an hour and a half splitting wood outside the woodshed flanking John Thunder's hotel. It felt good working with his shirt off, feeling the cooling late-afternoon and early evening air dry the sweat on his skin. It also felt good, after so long sitting a saddle, to work with his hands and arms, twisting and turning and stretching at the waist and shoulders, working out the kinks in his muscles.

So absorbed had he been in his work that when he'd put his shirt back on and walked around to the front of the hotel, he was surprised to see that several stout freight wagons had pulled up and were sitting in the yard, tongues slanting to the ground. The teams had been led away to a corral north of the hotel and where a good twenty or thirty stout mules stood munching hay out of freshly stocked cribs.

A bearded, sunburned gent was tending the mules—one of Thunder's hostlers, Yakima assumed. He must have been sleeping in the shed off the stable when Yakima and the girls had first arrived, just as Thunder's working girls, cook and bar tender had been sleeping upstairs in the hotel.

Yakima walked into the kitchen to find Thunder hustling up beans and steaks for the fifteen freighters lifting a loud, boisterous roar where they sat in the main drinking hall, swilling soapy mugs of ale that the bar tender, a tall, skinny gent in a bow tie and with a walrus mustache, was serving as fast as the freighters, speaking in various Scandinavian tongues, could empty the mugs. Thunder had a stout, middle-aged woman working in the kitchen, baking bread and washing dishes while John tended the stove.

Of course, Thunder's four doxies had come downstairs, brightly and scantily clad and were plying a brisk trade with the freighters.

Yakima helped out with the cooking of the steaks and beans and even assisted the woman, whose name was Gretta and who spoke with a German accent so heavy it was hard to understand her, roll out biscuit dough.

It was a long night, indeed. As empty as the building had been earlier, it was packed to the rafters intermittently all evening. When the freighters repaired to the stoop

215

with after-dinner glasses of schnaaps and cigars, their tables were taken by a pair of drummers and a half-dozen survey men and then by another half-dozen cow punchers just passing through with a herd they'd left out on the prairie in the care of a couple of nighthawks.

When the cowboys left to bed down with the cows, the two nighthawks—an older man and a tall, slender young man in his late teens—came in and polished off Thunder's stew and left. By that time, it was nearly eleven and the place had all but cleared out—most of the customers leaving the premises but a few having rented rooms upstairs for the night—save for a couple of freighters who'd pulled a single wagon up to the hotel around ten and were finishing up a pair of antelope steaks apiece and nursing creamy dark ales.

Yakima helped Gretta with the dishes while John stoked the stove and made another pot of coffee and then Greta, taking a break, sat down to a well-deserved meal of her own. Yakima and John ate together at the bar in the main saloon.

When they finished their meals and drinks and a friendly palaver over old times, John clapped Yakima on the shoulder and said, "I appreciate the help, old friend. You'd best head to bed. I know you want to get an early start in the mornin'. Me—I'm off to cut another haunch off one of the antelopes hanging in my keeper shed. We usually get a few more customers off the trail between midnight and when I lock up at one."

John left and Yakima stood alone at the bar, nursing one last ale and only absently listening to the rising din of hooves out in the yard again. The barman, whose name he'd learned was Luther, was switching kegs and restocking the shelves, which had nearly been depleted during the onslaught. Luther must have heard the sound of more approaching customers, as well, because as he pounded the bung starter into the new beer keg, he gave an audible groan.

Yakima had been hearing the din of conversations carried on in several different foreign tongues all night. He'd become inured to accents, which he was detecting from the yard now with only passing interest.

There came the thud of a single pair of boots on the stoop and then a woman's English-accented voice calling, "Oh, stop being so long in the face, Dottie. We're not *really* lost—we're just separated from the rest of the party for a time is all. I'm sure that when you regain your keen sense of direction as well as your stalwart male tracking abilities, we'll find the rest of the lads and lasses in the morning, and we'll all be one great big happy family again!"

Yakima looked with sudden interest in the backbar mirror to see a female figure clad in a long, fur coat and fur hat step through the saloon's front door. The woman, in her early twenties, removed the hat and swung her head to free the most beautiful tresses of rich chestnut hair Yakima had ever seen as she continued with: "All is not lost. Fortunately, we have stumbled upon this wonderful—"

She froze two steps inside the door, her radiant smile stiffening. Her gaze had found Yakima in the backbar mirror. As her thick hair settled about her shoulders in several radiantly messy piles, Yakima swung around to face her.

Instantly, his heart thudded. A second heart thudded deep in his loins.

Their eyes had met. His jade ones and hers—two frosty chunks of ice chipped from the deepest winter lake on the slopes of the highest Colorado mountain set in an oval-shaped face tooled to perfection and boasting a wide, erotic mouth complete with bee-stung lips that Yakima had a feeling were always shaped as though yearning for a deep, passionate kiss.

Her eyes, smoldering, bored into his.

Her chest rose and fell slowly, heavily. A slight flush rose in her perfect cheeks. Her mouth didn't move but her lips seemed to swell as she stood holding the half-breed's burning gaze with a desperate one of her own.

Another pair of boots thudded on the stoop and then a man's English-accented voice said, "Wait for me, please,

Bunnie. You mustn't enter these remote frontier establishments before I have had a chance to—"

Yakima had just caught sight of a white-bandaged nose and two swollen eyes over the radiant damsel's left shoulder before she wheeled to the man suddenly, grabbed the man's coat by its collar and swung him around to face her as she gave her back to the veranda. "My darling, look—you've gone and stained your new coat!" She brushed at the front of the coat with one hand while peeking around her husband at Yakima, lips pursed, her eyes wide with anxiety.

The beautiful waif was peering around none other than that insufferable popinjay, the Earl of Cork himself—William Anthony Boyle!

Anger burned in Yakima's loins as hot for the man as did his passion for the man's woman. Without even thinking, he found himself taking one step forward then reaching down to free the keeper thong from over the hammer of his .44.

The woman's eyes dropped to Yakima's hand. She shook her head, eyes glinting with shock and swept one arm toward the stairs.

Reluctantly, Yakima left the Colt in its holster, turned and headed for the stairs. He ordinarily never retreated from trouble, but he knew that if he remained here a moment longer, the earl was going to end up dead. While immensely satisfying, killing the duke would probably rush his trip to the gallows. Before he could shed these earthly shackles, he needed to get the girls to Cannon-ball as well as Cahill's letter and money to Paul's son at Fort Abercrombie.

"Oh, pooh," the earl's wife said with a pooch-mouthed pout, returning her attention to her broken-nosed charge. "Look, you've gone and ruined it. How are we ever going to—"

"Oh, darling, I think you're overreacting," said the Earl of Cork, glancing over his shoulder and frowning. "What are you looking at back there… whose…?"

The earl's eyes slid to the stairs just as Yakima climbed up out of the man's view.

"Oh, nobody, darling," Yakima heard the lady say as he moved down the hall toward his room. "I was just making sure the place was habitable, is all. You know how filthy these frontier places can be—and filled with such despicable characters!"

That was the last Yakima heard as he moved down the hall and stopped at the door of the girls' room. The woman was as haughty and smug as she was delightful to look at. He still felt the pounding in his loins that he'd felt when she'd first walked into the saloon, doffing that fur hat and shaking out all that hair.

He leaned close to the door, listening. No sounds

issued from the other side. The girls were sound asleep. They'd each had a long, hot bath and a hearty meal. After the long ride they'd so far endured, they'd sleep like logs all night. Yakima would probably have trouble rousing them in the morning.

He smiled as he stepped away from the door and headed for his own room one door down from the girls'. He used his key, went inside, lit a lamp and shucked out of his duds. He washed at the basin but didn't take the time to dry himself before he crawled naked into bed. He thought for sure he'd be out before his head hit the pillow.

No such luck.

Just behind his retinas flashed the beguiling face of the Earl of Cork's ravishing wife.

He wasn't sure how much time had passed when he woke from a doze. He lifted his head up, heart quickening. He'd heard something. It came again—the faint creak of a floorboard out in the hall.

Yakima grabbed his .44 from its holster just as a soft tap sounded on the door. He clicked the hammer back.

"Who is it?" he grunted.

The only response was one more soft tap.

Yakima wrinkled a brow as he pondered the door. One of the girls?

Or trouble?

He threw his bedcovers aside, sat up and lit the hurricane lamp on the small table beside his bed. He rose and walked slowly to the door, keeping the cocked Colt aimed at it. Keeping to the door's left side, he tipped his head to the wall and asked again, a little louder this time:

"Who is it?"

A very low but tense voice said, "Let me in."

It sounded like a female voice. Might be Annie but he didn't think so. Since there was a chance it was Annie and because she and Beth might be in trouble, he turned the key in the lock, twisted the knob and opened it four inches, peering through it with one eye and keeping the .44 leveled on it.

Two gray eyes stared at him from between thick tresses of rich, dark hair that glistened in the moonlight angling through a hall window, from inside the hood of the black cape she wore. The Earl of Cork's wife shoved the door open with one hand and took two quick steps into the room.

Yakima was so flummoxed at seeing her here that he did nothing to stop her. He looked at her dumbly, jaw hanging. She smiled up at him then set one hand against the door and very quietly closed and latched it.

"Uh…" was all Yakima could say, slowly lowering the Colt to his side.

She crossed her arms and lifted the cape up over her head. She tossed it onto a chair. Yakima sucked a sharp breath as her thick hair settled back down over her shoulders and curled around her large, pale breasts.

She wasn't wearing a stitch. Naked as the day she was born but a whole lot better filled out.

"I've always wanted to sleep with a red man," she said and shoved him toward the bed.

Chapter 20

"Gwen-do-lynnn?"

The screeching cry plucked Yakima out of a deep sleep.

It awakened the Earl of Cork's wife, as well. Yakima found her lying against him. The covers were pulled down, nearly exposing them both. She lifted her head and the messy tresses of her hair danced about her neck and shoulders and gently caressed Yakima's belly, like threads of fine silk.

She blinked and looked around, still half-asleep, trying to get her bearings.

"GWEN-DOLL-YNNN?" came the screech again, louder this time. "Where are you—damn you? I know you're behind one of these doors. Get out here this instant, you slattern! The man you are with is going to get a *bullet!*"

The earl's wife gasped and closed her hand over her

mouth. "Oh, my good Lord—what am I still doing in here?"

Late dawn light with a good bit of early sunshine angled in through the curtained window to Yakima's left, her right. The footsteps in the hall grew louder, the voice even crazier with anguish. "Gwendolyn—bloody hell, why have you done this to me? Cuckolded me again in front of the whole world?"

Squinting his eyes against the light, Yakima looked at her through his own mussed hair. "Are you Gwendolyn?" They hadn't exchanged names last night though that was about the only thing they had not exchanged.

She gazed wide-eyed down at Yakima then glanced at the door. "Boy, he's really on a tear this morning!"

"You promised!" The earl stomped a foot down hard on the hall floor. "You promised you would never do this to me again!"

Gwendolyn scrambled off of Yakima and then off of the bed. He watched with a constriction in his throat and a fluttery heart as she bent forward to pick the cape up off the floor. An incredible view the likes of which he would doubtless remember on his deathbed.

Voices and rumblings rose in the other rooms around Yakima. The Earl of Cork was awakening the entire hotel. Now he seemed to be sobbing as he strode with irregular footsteps along the hall. A loud banging rose as he knocked on a door. "Are you in there? Are you in there, Gwendolyn—damn your cheating heart!"

"Hey, knock it off out there or I'll carve out *your* heart, bucko!" came a muffled male shout from a room on the other side of the hall.

"Is my wife in there, you lout?" the earl shouted. "I will shoot the man who has cuckolded me, Gwendolyn!"

Yakima reached for his Colt, pulled it from his holster then lay back against his pillow.

Gwendolyn let the cape drop down over her pretty, naked pink body, threw her hair out from behind the collar and looked at Yakima. "Please don't shoot him. He's a simple fool as well as impotent, but you have no idea how much money he's worth!"

She blew Yakima a kiss and opened the door. She started to step through it when she saw that before her stood none other than the Earl of Cork himself, hand raised, ready to pound.

Gwendolyn gasped, tensing.

Sir William Anthony Boyle's mouth and eyes grew wide, his eyes nearly as wide as his mouth despite the swelling around them. His bandaged nose glowed.

"*Ah-hahh!* Caught you red-handed!"

"Oh, no you didn't, Doddie. We finished *hours* ago. I was just so sated I fell asleep." She glanced at Yakima over her shoulder and winked.

"Trollop!" Berated the earl. He shoved her aside and stepped into the room, holding the silver-chased, pearl gripped pocket revolver down low by his right side. "And you, sir—"

He stopped when his eyes found Yakima's large, brawny, copper-skinned body lounging on the bed, holding his own revolver in his hand. Yakima held it in his right hand, that arm draped casually over his right, upraised knee. "*You!*" he wailed. "You! Who broke my nose! You filthy savage…and then you have the gall to befoul my wife?"

The rail-thin gent clad in a silk nightgown under a red velvet, monogrammed bathrobe, still held his fancy popper down by his side. That's why Yakima kept his own hogleg hanging down over his knee.

"The befouling of your wife was her idea—not mine!"

"It's true, Doddie! What do you expect me to do? I have to go *somewhere* for my comforts!" Gwendolyn tugged on the dandy's arm. "Come hither—we must get back to our room for baths!"

"Yeah—come hither," said a deep, raspy male voice from somewhere in the hall.

Yakima could see three burly freighters standing on the far side of the hall, flanking the earl and his wife. They all were dressed in grubby longhandles and looked recently roused from sleep, but the expressions on their faces were those of men enjoying a good show at the local opera house on a hopping Saturday night. Doubtless the hall was filled with spectators though Yakima couldn't see them from inside his room. The freighters he could see laughed at the comment, glancing down the hall to their left. So did a few women—likely Thunder's percentage gals, also awakened by the foofaraw.

"No, no, no—this filthy savage is not going to get away with this!"

"He already did and I assure you I'll be in the best of moods for the rest of our journey!"

More laughter in the hall.

Still tugging on her husband's arm, Gwendolyn flashed Yakima a devilish smirk.

Pulling his arm loose of his wife's grip, the earl barked at Yakima, "You, sir, will die like the cur you are!"

As he raised his pretty pocket pistol, Yakima raised and aimed his .44 from over his bare right knee. "You level that little popper on me, you're a dead man. I will splatter your brains all over the men behind you!"

That caused the freighters to wince and shuffle out of the line of fire.

"Doddie!" Gwendolyn leaped on her husband's right shoulder, pulling his gun hand down. "Doddie, you're no match for him. Take it from me—he's a lion! He will kill you!"

"Let me go…let me go, damn you, wife—I have my pride!"

He fought to raise the gun but it appeared he was no match for his wife, who kept leaping at him, pulling his gun hand down and tugging on his arm, trying to drag him back to their room.

Yakima held his Colt steady on the little Irishman. He didn't want to kill him for Gwendolyn's sake. After the unexpected fun she'd provided for him, he supposed he owed her the favor of not shooting her moneyed husband, but his patience was wearing thin. If that fancy little hogleg was aimed at him, he'd take the shot. He had to defend himself.

Surely, they couldn't hang him for defending himself—even if he was defending himself against an earl! They probably would, though, him being a half-breed. Still, he would by god defend himself.

"Doddie—no—give—me—*that!*" Gwendolyn struggled with the earl. She was trying to pry the man's fingers free of the gun. Bent forward and to one side, the Irishman fought stubbornly to maintain his grip.

"Oh, fer chrissakes," Yakima said.

He dropped his feet to the floor, rose from the bed, wrapped a sheet around himself, knotted it at his waist and walked over to where the pair was fighting in the doorway. Yakima smacked the barrel of his pistol against the back of the earl's head. Not a skull crusher but a little more than a love tap.

The earl groaned and dropped straight down to the floor.

"There you go," Yakima told the lady. "He's all yours. Best get him out of here before I have to beef him."

The earl was only partly out. He lay on his side, groaning and cursing.

Gwendolyn smiled at Yakima. "Thank you."

"Don't mention it."

"Come on, Doddie," she said, crouching and trying to pull her husband to his feet. "Let's let you get back in bed. Time for a little tea and some Spanish brandy, I think."

When she finally got the swooning earl to his feet and led him off down the hall, the earl leaning against her and shuffling his slippered feet, the other men in the hall as well as the parlor girls clapped and whistled.

Yakima stepped back and was about to close the door when Annie and Beth stepped into his doorway, staring up at him. He winced. He also flushed. He'd be damned if in all the commotion he hadn't forgotten about his two young charges residing right next door to him.

Yakima hummed, hawed, conscious of his bare chest, the sheet around his waist. The gun in his hand. The badly rumpled bed behind him.

The unseemliness of the whole affair came home to

him in the gazes of the two girls standing hand in hand, staring up at him. No judge had ever given him as castigating a look. They mixed a good bit of disappointment into that look, as well, and that's what bit him the deepest.

Yakima opened and closed his mouth in frustration, trying to find words. Finally, he said, "That feller and me have history!"

Beth's eyes sharpened as she said snidely, "Well, now you have history with his wife, too, don't you?"

Yakima flinched. The little girl's words were a slap across the face.

Annie said, "We're packed up and heading downstairs for breakfast." She dropped her eyes to the sheet. "It is morning, you know." She and Beth gave him one more pointed look then turned away and walked down the hall toward the stairs.

Yakima stood in the open doorway, lower jaw hanging. His guts felt like charred ash. He felt like gutter trash.

They'd seen and heard the whole thing. Oh, well. Maybe just as well they saw him, warts and all. He was just a man. Not the best. Certainly, not the worst.

Certainly not the best, either.

"Ah, hell," he said in resignation, and slammed the door. "Women."

***

After Yakima had gone downstairs and joined the two girls for a breakfast of flapjacks, bacon, eggs and fried potatoes as well as a tall glass of fresh milk from John Thunder's cow, he and the girls thanked John for his hospitality. Yakima and the big half-breed shared a brief, stiff but heartfelt hug in the yard, knowing they might not see each other again for another few years, and that, the frontier being what it was and they the men they were, they might not see each other again at all. Yakima and the girls mounted up and continued their journey north, on the last stretch of trail to Cannonball.

In fact, they should reach the town by sundown the next day. This would be their last full day together on the trail. Yakima wasn't sure how he felt about that. Even given the trouble they were, he'd grown fond of his young trail pards. Just like after Paul had died down in New Mexico, he'd be lonely without them.

But, then, he'd gotten used to loneliness a long time ago.

"You girls lookin' forward to seein' your grandparents, are ya?" Yakima asked as they rode. So far, they hadn't spoken much since the embarrassing incident earlier in Thunder's hotel.

"I am," Beth said from her customary perch behind her sister. "As long as they'll take us," she added a little sourly. "I think Gram would take us in right quick, but Gramps can be kinda notional. Our ma always called him notional. Doesn't like kids much. Kind of a grouch. Doesn't like the messes they make."

"How 'bout you, Annie?"

Annie did not respond. She continued riding the chestnut with her head pointed forward, face sullen beneath the floppy brim of her bullet-crowned felt hat.

"Annie?" Yakima prodded her.

"She's mad at you," Beth said with a smirk. "She's *jealous!*"

Annie twisted around in her saddle to give her sister a caustic glare. "I am not *jealous!*" She turned to Yakima. "I'm repulsed!" She crinkled up her nose at him then turned her head forward again to stare out over her horse's twitching ears.

"I'm sorry I disappointed you, Annie."

Again, she did not respond.

Beth turned to Yakima grinning and mouthing the word: "Jealous."

Yakima sighed and continued the journey across the nearly featureless fawn prairie spread out around them to the far horizon. The only notable landmarks were occasional creeks and dry washes scored shallowly in the sandy soil and occasional haystack buttes lifting their bullet-nosed heads in the hazy pale distance.

This was coyote and rattlesnake country, prickly pear and sage brush country, and not much else.

Occasionally they'd pass a few cows idly cropping grass. Once, a little after noon, Yakima saw a couple cow punchers slowly, deliberately herding a handful of cow-calf pairs along a dry wash, whooping and clucking and whistling and waving their coiled lariats. They were a good distance off and headed northeast, likely to some home ranch out that way. No doubt a lonely place, indeed.

Yakima hipped around in his saddle to cast his gaze behind him, along the long, pale, winding ribbon of their backtrail. He realized that he'd done the same thing a good five or six times in the past five minutes.

Why?

He halted Wolf with a soft "Whoa," and curveted the horse to gaze more carefully across the country they'd just traversed—a gently rolling ocean of dun grass and lime-colored sage, with occasional knife slashes of mostly dry ravines. Annie and Beth rode ahead a few more steps before Annie glanced at Yakima then stopped and curveted the chestnut, as well.

"What is it?"

"I don't know. I got this vague notion we got us a shadow."

Chapter 21

Yakima leaned back to reach into a saddlebag pouch for his spy glass. He extended the piece and adjusted the focus.

He swept the landscape behind thoroughly, slowly sliding the glass from left to right, right to left. He scoured a jog of low, chalky buttes to the southwest and saw only a coyote trotting along its shoulder, some dead animal drooping from its jaws, probably a rabbit.

"Nothin'."

He looked around, saw a hill about a hundred yards off the trail to the northwest. Glancing at the girls, he said, "Wait here."

He gigged the black through short brome and needlegrass and around a large patch of prickly pear. When he'd climbed to within a few feet of the crest of the hill, he stopped Wolf and raised the spy glass again. Again, he gave his and the girls' trail a very close survey.

Still seeing nothing—only two white-tail does leading a late-year fawn across a dry wash straight south, the fawn suddenly breaking into a buck-kicking run ahead of the two older deer, shaking its head wildly, just having fun.

Yakima returned the spy glass to his saddlebags then rode back down to where the girls waited atop the chestnut, their eyes cast with concern.

"Nothing," he said. "I'll keep a close eye out, but sometimes that sixth sense of mine sings without a fiddle. There's a stream another click or so ahead, a higher bluff alongside it. We'll water the horses there and I'll climb the bluff for a better look. If there's anybody trailin' us, I'll be able to see him from there."

Beth nodded.

Annie only shrugged a shoulder.

Still mad at him.

He felt bad that Annie was mad at him. He'd been an idiot to do what he'd done last night, but he was a man, after all, with a man's urges and he hadn't enjoyed a woman's flesh for a long, dry stretch though he'd be damned if he hadn't been tempted.

Still, he didn't like Annie being mad. He hoped she'd come around before they reached her and Beth's grandparents' place. He didn't want them to part on bad terms.

When they reached the stream, which was sheathed in large cottonwoods and shrubs, Yakima and Wolf led the girls down the slope through the trees. He stopped at the edge of the wide, sun-lit water, dismounted and helped Annie and Beth from the chestnut's back. He loosened the saddle cinch of both horses, so they could rest and drink freely.

"Why don't you two fill your canteen? Fill mine while you're at it, will you?" Yakima shucked the Yellowboy from his saddle scabbard and once again fished his spy glass out of his saddlebag pouch. "I'm gonna climb that bluff yonder."

He canted his head toward a high, steep, sandstone ridge capped with loose chunks of red rock.

"I'll fill your canteen for you, Yakima," Beth said, rising on her tiptoes to free the lanyard from his saddlehorn.

Annie had already turned away to fill her and Beth's own canteen at the stream.

"Thank you, my dear," Yakima said, giving Beth a wink.

He glanced at Annie. She kept her back to him in a very cold and meaningful way. She was a handful that one. At first glance, you might think Beth was the one who'd give no quarter. Not true. Annie was the toughest of the pair. She could be the most unforgiving and uncompromising.

Not that he deserved forgiveness, but he wished she'd forgive him. Or at least understand him.

The trouble, he knew, was that she thought she was in love with him. He'd callously hurt her last night and she was making him pay the price for it, wanting to wound him at least half as deep as he'd wounded her.

"You damn fool," he muttered to himself, walking away from the girls and the horses with his Winchester in his hand.

***

Annie finished filling the canteen and capped it.

As she did, she looked up to see Beth wading out into the stream. The girl had taken her shoes and socks off; they lay behind her at the edge of the shore, socks stuffed into the shoes.

"Beth, what are you doing?"

Beth kept walking, very slowly heading for the opposite shore, head down, arms held out to both sides for balance.

"What's it look like?" she said, customarily snooty. "I'm cooling my feet."

"You be careful. Don't get swept away by the current, Beth."

"I won't. The water's not very deep."

The water appeared to be up around her knees. Beth had raised her skirt high, revealing her pantaloons, which she also pushed up on her legs.

"Don't go far."

"I won't, worry wart."

Annie turned away from the stream. There were plenty of trees and shrubs along the shore. She stepped into some shrubs on the far side of a large, round rock. She pulled her bloomers and pantaloons down, squatted and made water.

She thought about Yakima. Hurt burned in her. She knew it shouldn't, but it did.

She rose, pulled her bloomers up, dropped her skirt and stepped out of the bushes. She looked for Beth. The stream was empty. Annie's heart lurched, skipped a beat, then settled down when she saw Beth on the opposite bank, about ten feet up from the water. She was pulling berries off what appeared a raspberry shrub.

"Now what are you doing?" Annie called to her sister across the stream in exasperation.

"Picking berries!" Beth said, turning to face Annie, showing her red lips as she chewed.

"Beth we're not going to be here that long—" Annie stopped suddenly when a large, black-clad man stepped out from a clump of bushes just above where Beth was picking berries.

He was a gray-haired, gray-mustached man dressed all in black. He appeared a specter from a nightmare. Gasping, Annie blinked her eyes as if to clear them of the image she could only be imagining.

The specter dropped quickly down the slope toward Beth.

He was headed straight for Beth!

Beth couldn't see him because she was partly turned away from him. He came down the slope on her right side and circled around behind her. He moved quickly, raising and spreading his arms—a monster loosed from hell to wreak havoc on little girls, his face shaping an expression of wide-eyed evil and maliciousness!

Annie lurched forward, gave a garbled wail, and tripped over a rock.

She fell and looked up just as the nightmare specter wrapped his arms around Beth and lifted her up off the ground.

"*Beth!*" Annie wailed.

Beth screamed as the man drew her taut against him then swung around and ran back up the slope, Annie kicking and screaming in his arms.

"Annie!" Beth screamed.

"Beth!" Annie wailed again, heaving herself to her feet, panic making her heavy and confused.

She watched in utter shock and horror as the black-cloaked nightmare specter ran up the hill with her sister in his arms. He pushed through shrubs and was gone, the sun-washed branches bouncing back into place, marking his passing.

Gone, gone! Beth was gone!

Chapter 22

"Yak-i-mahhhh!"

Yakima lowered the spy glass and stared down the hill beyond Wolf, toward the trees along the creek in which he'd left Annie and Beth. Wolf whickered and turned his head to peer in the same direction.

"Yak-i-mahhhh!" came Annie's sobbing wail once more.

Yakima lurched to his feet. He stuffed the spyglass into his saddlebag pouch, leaped into the saddle, and booted Wolf down the hill at a hard gallop.

Again, Annie screamed his name.

Wolf raced toward the trees, Yakima crouched low in the saddle. He slowed the stallion as they moved through the trees and shrubs and then he saw the dark-brown stream and Annie kneeling on the shore, sobbing, lifting her head once more to scream his name.

"I'm here!" he said as Wolf burst out of the trees. Yakima stopped the mount and leaped out of the saddle to kneel beside Annie, whose face was ashen and tear-streaked. "What happened?"

"Beth!"

Yakima looked around. "Where is she?"

Annie turned and pointed up the hill on the opposite side of the stream. "H-he h-he *took* her! A man came down the hill. He was dressed in black! Beth was picking berries. He grabbed her and rushed up the hill with her! Oh, Yakima, it was horrible. She's *gone!*"

"Wait here!"

Yakima again leaped up onto Wolf's back and booted horse into the stream and across to the other side. Wolf lunged up the opposite bank. Yakima steered him toward where he could see the bent grass forming a trail around raspberry shrubs and straight up the hill beyond them. He followed the trail to the hill's crest and looked around wildly, his heart racing. Cottonwoods towered over him, striping the grass at the top of the hill with shadows.

Looking around carefully, his right hand on his gun butt, he rode north along the hill that sloped gradually downward. The grass was thinner up here around patches of sand and gravel. His gaze landed on a pile of fresh horse apples and then he saw the prints of where a shod horse had stood, likely tied to a tree.

He rode forward, casting his gaze along the ground. Picking up the trail of the horse heading down the north side of the hill, he followed it, looking ahead and to both sides but keeping his eyes on the tracks so he didn't lose the kidnapper's trail. He followed the trail through scattered cedars and pines and on down the hill.

Another, steeper hill rose on his left. Yet another rose just to the right of the first one, its crest set a little farther back and capped with more pines and cedars as well as one large cottonwood whose bright yellow leaves littered the ground at its base.

Yakima drew sharply back on Wolf's reins when he saw the horse at the top of the hill. It was a silver bay, its mane so bleached it appeared nearly white against the horse's copper coat. The mount stood facing him in front of the cottonwood and the yellow carpet the tree had made of its leaves.

Yakima's heart lurched hopefully when he saw Beth sitting in the horse's saddle. But then it lurched again, this time dreadfully, when he saw the noose around her neck and the rope angling straight up above her head and around a stout branch eight feet straight above the girl. The end of the rope was tied low on the tree's other side.

Yakima whipped his hand back to pluck his spy glass from his saddlebag pouch. Extending it, he raised it quickly and adjusted the focus until Beth and the copper bay swam into view. Beth sat the horse sobbing, her hands apparently tied behind her back. The bay's reins were tied around the horn.

"No," Yakima grunted. "No, no, no, no!"

He lowered the glass, resisting the urge to gallop up the hill. The bay was free and Beth's hands were tied behind her back. If that horse moved more than a few feet, Beth would hang.

Heart racing, Yakima raised the glass once more. He scanned the area around Beth.

"Come on, Reverend," Yakima said through gritted teeth. "I know it's you, you damn coward! Show yourself, you gutless cur. Using a little girl to draw me into a trap!"

Seeing no sign of the man who's doing this was, Yakima lowered the glass and slid down from the saddle. He moved slowly. He was a hundred yards away from Beth and the silver bay, but he was so keenly aware that the bay was free to roam as it pleased and could spook at any time—by Yakima, by a bird, even by just a falling pine cone—that he felt as though lead had replaced the marrow in his bones.

One too sudden of a move and Beth would hang.

If he walked up there, the horse would likely spook.

If he did not walk up there and free the girl, the horse would also eventually spook or just drift off to graze or look for water.

Knowing he had no choice but to take the chance, Yakima walked forward, automatically holding his hands up, palms out in supplication to the horse. He had to try and get up there before the horse moved.

He took one step, two steps, three...

Staring down the slope at Yakima, the horse twitched its left ear.

Yakima froze.

"Yakima!" a girl yelled behind him beneath with the thud of trotting hooves.

He sucked a breath through gritted teeth and whipped around to see Annie riding up behind him on the chestnut.

He held both hands straight out in front of him, palms out, keeping her back.

Annie reined up, frowning curiously.

"Stay right there and don't move," he raked out in breathless desperation. "Beth is up there with a rope around her neck."

Annie's lower jaw dropped and she closed her hand over her mouth as she stared past Yakima at the silver bay on the hill beyond him.

Yakima turned back to face the hill and the horse and the girl with the rope around her neck. The bay watched him closely, one ear bent slightly forward.

Yakima moved ahead slowly, setting each mocca-sin-clad foot down as though he were walking on thin ice that creaked and groaned beneath his every step. He suppressed his almost overwhelming urge to run. If he ran, the bay would bolt. He wanted to call out to the ruthless Reverend and beg for Beth's mercy, but his voice, too, would likely frighten the bay into movement.

The last time he'd felt such deep frustration was when he'd held his dead bride in his arms, powerless to do anything for her.

He moved ahead one step at a time. He knew it was likely the Reverend would kill him before he reached the bay, but he had no choice but to try. If he did nothing, Beth would die. She still might very well die, but at least he would have tried to save her.

He discovered now that he treasured the girl so much that he didn't mind at all giving his own life to save hers.

Another step…another…another…

He was fifty yards away from Beth, climbing the hill toward her and the horse. So far, the bay had not moved other than to turn its head to look at something to its right, probably a bird moving among the branches. It turned its head back forward to watch the big man moving toward him and twitched its left ear, listening, sniffing, trying to detect if the approaching man meant danger.

"Easy," Yakima said. "I mean you no harm, horse."

He could clearly see Beth's eyes on him now. Her lips

trembled and tears bathed her pale face.

She knew not to squirm around, not to cry out.

A brave child. Most would have screamed by now.

Not Beth. No. You could depend on Beth when the chips were down.

The question was could she depend on Yakima?

Moving slowly up the steepest part of the hill now, Yakima closed to within forty yards…

The horse shifted a front foot, whickered, turned its head askance. It gave Yakima a wary look.

"Whoa, boy…whoa, boy…"

"Thirty…"

The horse sidestepped to the right. No longer able to contain her horror, Beth gave a strangled wail as the rope drew her sideways, canting her head to one side, stretching out every bit of slack in the rope.

Yakima stopped suddenly. He'd spied movement directly behind the tree before which Beth sat atop the jittery bay. He'd caught a glimpse of a black hat brim poking out from behind the tree, on its left side. He'd also glimpsed the end of a rifle barrel.

There was no more time. In maybe one…two seconds, he'd be dead.

He had only one option. He had no choice but to try.

Lightning-quick, he drew the .44 from its holster, cocked it, raised it high and narrowed one eye as he aimed in desperation at the rope stretched taut above the girl's head. The Colt roared as in the corner of his left eye he watched the black-clad Reverend step out from behind the tree and raise a rifle to his shoulder.

His Colt's report was followed closely by two more gun reports. One was slightly ahead of the second report, which was much louder than that of the first, because it came from the Reverend's rifle. The second crack—really more of a loud roar—was accompanied by orange flames and smoke lapping from the Reverend's gun.

Yakima was only vaguely aware of these two other reports.

At the moment he watched in horror as the silver bay wheeled sharply to its left and galloped off, Beth sliding off the saddle to hang suspended in the air over where the saddle had just been a second ago. Screaming, she dropped slightly; Yakima had shot halfway through the rope and the last strands were quickly unravelling.

Staying as still as stone though for the life of him he didn't how he managed it under such circumstances, he aimed again, fired again. Time had slowed to a crawl, but his shots were probably only separated by one and a half seconds. His second bullet sliced through the last strands of the rope and Beth fell to pile up on the ground with a thump and a loud grunt.

Yakima pivoted to his left.

The Reverend was on the ground, bleeding from his chest. He'd lost his hat. His head was bald save for a band of short gray hair above his ears. He started to raise his Henry rifle again, his eyes startled, bewildered.

Stretching gray-mustached lips back from his teeth, he slid the barrel of the rifle toward Yakima, who shot him three times, punching two rounds through his forehead and only about two inches apart and another through his throat.

The Reverend flopped back with a startled grunt, dead as toast.

Yakima hurried forward and dropped to a knee beside Beth who had sat up with a startled look, looking around nearly as bewilderedly as the Reverend just had, then opened her mouth and eyes wide and wailed. Yakima glanced behind him to see Annie galloping the chestnut up the hill. She was still holding Yakima's Winchester in her hand, laid across her saddle pommel.

He turned to Beth, sandwiched the child's face in his hands, and titled it up toward his. "Are you all right, darlin'? He didn't hurt you too bad, did he?"

Beth's wails turned to sobs. She squeezed her eyes closed, shook her head, and threw her arms around Yakima, burying her face in his chest, clinging to him desperately, her little body jerking as she cried.

Annie drew the chestnut to a skidding halt. "Oh, Beth!"

Annie hurried over, handed the Yellowboy to Yakima and knelt beside him and her sister. "Are you all right, Beth? Dear, Lord, I was so frightened!"

Beth peeled herself away from Yakima and flung herself at her sister, wrapping her arms tightly around the older girl's neck. "I'm all right, Annie! I was so...I was so *scared!*"

She sobbed against Annie's chest. Annie hugged her tightly, rocking her gently. She rested her chin on Beth's head and looked at Yakima. "Nice shootin'."

"Same to you." Yakima shook his head incredulously. "How did you ever make that shot?"

"I told you Pa taught me how to protect Ma and Beth. I wasn't able to do much for Ma, but I was bound and determined to help Beth!" She smiled and kissed the top of her sister's head. "I knew what you were going to do. I had it figured right. I'm sorry about how I acted—you know—earlier...about that woman."

"You got pluck, girl," Yakima said, clamping his hand against the back of her neck.

"Truth to tell, I wasn't sure I could make that shot. Especially with a strange gun, an' all. But I shucked it and propped it on a rock. I was sure that savage would see me step around Wolf and grab the rifle, but I still had to try. By then I knew he was fixing to shoot you, so I figured I could take the chance he had both eyes on you. I knew he had you to dead to rights and you and Beth would die if I didn't do something."

Tears glazed her eyes and she shook her head slowly. "I wanted to just curl up and die but I had to do something!"

"You did something, all right."

"Who was that…if you and the Good Lord will forgive my blue tongue…*rotten bastard?*"

"Bounty hunter."

"Figures."

Yakima winced, shook his head, reached out to caress Beth's tear-damp cheek with his thumb. "I almost got you both killed with my fool ways. Stoppin' in Deadwood. That's where the Reverend came from."

"No." Annie shook her head determinedly. "You saved our lives, Yakima."

He thought about that. He smiled and nodded. "And you and Beth have done the same thing for me."

Holding Beth, Annie slid over and kissed Yakima's shoulder and snuggled luxuriously up against the big man's thick arm.

Chapter 23

The next day when the shadows were growing long, Yakima, Annie, and Beth turned off the main trail onto a secondary two-track trail. They rode through some cottonwoods and crossed a creek. When they emerged from one more grove of leafless cottonwoods, a handsome farmyard spread out before them complete with a two-story clapboard house with a broad front porch with a picturesque red clapboard barn and several other outbuildings flanking it. Smoke curled from the brick chimney running up the house's east side.

The yard was large and surrounded by harvested wheat and corn fields. Two apple trees stood in the yard, to either side of the cobblestone path that led up from the circular gravel drive. The apples, too, had been long since harvested.

It was a crisp autumn day, but the sun cast a lemon

glow onto the house's steeply pitched roof. The front yard was in shadow, for the sun was dropping down behind the house and the barn. Over the yard lay the savory smell of cooked pot roast and gravy and the cinnamon of an apple pie.

Yakima reined up at the end of the leaf-littered cobblestone path and glanced at Annie who drew rein beside him. "This the place, ladies?"

"Yep," Annie said with a fateful air. "This is the place."

Footsteps sounded from inside the house, behind the front door, which was propped two-feet open with a brick, likely to let the heat from the evening's cooking out. "Someone's here, mother," came a man's voice. "I'm going to see who it—" The man stopped as he shoved the door farther open and poked his bald head out, scowling.

Yakima figured the man must see quite the unlikely image—one big red man in buckskins and two young white girls.

"What the…?" The man, tall and lean and bespectacled, somewhere in his sixties and with a bushy mustache set beneath a long, ship's prow nose, stepped tentatively onto the porch, holding the door as though clinging to a life raft on stormy seas. He wore a wool work shirt and overalls. A briar pipe jutted from a front pocket of the overalls.

Yakima saw the girls tense beside him. He thought he

heard Beth draw a sharp breath.

"Mr. Magnusson?" Yakima asked.

The man didn't say anything for a moment but only blinked as he regarded the unlikely scene before him. Finally, he said, "What is it?"

"I'm Yakima Henry." Yakima canted his head toward the girls sitting the chestnut beside him. "These are your granddaughters."

The man's severe brows ridged even more severely as he switched his gaze back to the girls. "They...are...?"

"Yes, sir. They've had a bit of trouble."

The man turned his head to call into the house: "Mother, you'd better come out here!"

"What is it?" came a woman's voice from within.

"Come out here, Marion!"

Heavy footsteps rose from inside the house. The man took a step to one side as a portly, buxom woman in a flowered dress and apron poked her gray head out the door, frowning. "What is...?"

She let her voice trail off when she saw the girls. Her frown deepened. She stepped out onto the porch and moved slowly forward, studying the girls. When she stopped at the top of the porch steps, deep lines gullied her pale, fleshy forehead as she said, "Annie? *Beth?*"

"Hello, Grams," Annie said, and slid her gaze to the stern-looking man standing beside Grams. "Hello,

Gramps."

Beth said nothing. She just looked silently around from behind her sister, a wary, cautious expression on her sunburned features.

Lower jaw hanging, Grams turned to Gramps.

Yakima felt his heart pick up speed with the dreaded anticipation of the girls' rejection by their grandparents.

But then the old woman turned back to Annie and Beth and exclaimed, "*Good Lord!*" She hitched her long skirts up above her ankle boots as she dropped quickly though heavily and haltingly down the porch steps. She hurried into the yard, her ample bosoms jouncing inside the floral day dress she wore. "Oh, Good Lord—I've been so worried!" she fairly howled. She glanced over her shoulder at Gramps. "*We've* been so worried!"

"Oh, dear." Gramps came ambling down the steps, as well, and strode quickly to the girls, who glanced at each other, hope growing in their eyes.

They turned to Yakima and he returned their relieved smiles with a relieved one of his own.

He swung down from Wolf's back, hurried over and helped both girls down from the chestnut's back just in time for Grams to wrap her arms around Annie, fairly engulfing the girl in her big, fleshy arms and mountainous bosom. Hugging Annie, she wrapped one arm around Beth and drew the smaller girl to her, as well. "I was so worried! I was so worried!" the old woman cried, hugging her granddaughters close.

She pulled away from the girls to look at Annie and then at Beth, tears streaming down her fleshy cheeks. "I didn't know what would happen after Alice died. I wrote to Henricks several times, but he never wrote me back!" She looked at the old man, who came up to stand a tentative way back but with a frown of concern on his craggy features. "He never wrote back! We were both so worried—Gramps, too!"

Annie was crying, now, too, with relief, Yakima could tell from where he stood back against the side of his horse, as relieved as the girls were to see that they'd been welcomed with open arms. Beth wasn't crying but she gazed up at her grandmother with an open-mouthed smile.

Upper lip trembling, Annie said, "He was awful, Grams. I won't tell you what he did, but it was awful. I beaned him with a bottle and me an' Beth ran!"

Grams gasped, then covered her mouth to stifle a laugh. "Oh, you did!"

"Knocked him flat out!" said Beth.

"Oh, you did!" exclaimed Gramps, also cracking a smile.

"Can we stay with you, Grams, Gramps?" Beth asked hopefully. "We don't have nowhere else to go!"

"Why, of course, you can, dear!" Grams said. "Can't they, Gramps?"

"Of course, of course," the old man said, smiling and nodding. He canted his head toward the house's second story. "We still have your ma's old room and Uncle Lyle's. They're both just gatherin' dust with no one to use 'em. I guess that means you can each have your own room and now Mother will have help in the kitchen and I"—he glanced pointedly but with humor at Beth—"will have help milking cows in the barn!"

They laughed. Annie covered her mouth, sobbing joyfully. She stepped out away from her grandmother and Beth and walked toward Yakima, extending her hand to him. "Grams, Gramps, I want you to meet our new friend, Yakima Henry." She stood beside him, pressing her right arm against his left one. "He saved us from the Hat Creek Stage Station. He took us under his wing and led us all this way!"

Annie rose up onto her toes and pressed her lips to Yakima's cheek.

Both Gram and Gramps had turned to study the big red man uncertainly.

Yakima smiled and doffed his hat. "Ma'am," he said, nodding at Grams. "Sir," he said, nodding at Gramps. "Your granddaughters are a rare delight. I'm just happy to see they got a new home."

"Mister Henry," Ma said, smiling benevolently at Yakima. "We are in the middle of supper, me an' Gramps.

Come join us and the girls for a hearty meal. We have so much to thank you for."

"I don't think so, ma'am," Yakima said, stepping forward and brushing bits of weed seeds from the crown of his hat. He glanced at Annie and Beth. "I think I'm gonna leave the four of you alone to get reacquainted. Besides, there's still enough light left for me to get a few more clicks on up the trail. I'm headed over to eastern Dakota, you see." He canted his head in that direction.

"Oh, Yakima!" Annie objected. "Do join us!"

"Join us, Yakima," Beth agreed.

"I don't think so, girls. I think I'll just say good-bye here an' now, an' mosey along." Why delay the inevitable?

Yakima looked at Annie. She gazed up at him frowning sadly. So was Beth. Yakima smiled at them both and set his hat back on his head.

"In that case," Grams said, breaking the awkward silence, "Gramps and I will go on inside. We'll leave you three to say your proper good-byes." She strode over to the old man and hooked her arm through his. "Come along, Gramps."

"All right, Mother."

Yakima turned to the two girls standing before him. He sighed, stepped forward, knelt in front of Beth, and wrapped the girl in his arms.

"I'm going to miss you, Yakima," Beth said.

"Me, too, kid," he said, pulling away from her.

"Thank you for takin' us to Gram and Gramps."

He smiled. "Any time."

"I wish you could stay with us. Maybe…"

"Nah, I don't think so, honey." Yakima shook his head slowly. "My home is that horse an' that saddle."

Beth planted a kiss on his cheek and said with a forlorn air, "Good-bye."

"Good-bye, honey."

Yakima rose to find Annie looking at him with tears in her eyes. A couple grew large, spilled out of her eyes, and dribbled down her cheeks.

"No tears, honey," Yakima said, swabbing her cheeks with his thumbs.

He planted a warm kiss on her forehead. A lump had grown in his throat. He held his lips against Annie's forehead. When he pulled away, she lurched toward him, wrapped her arms around him and buried her face in his chest, sobbing.

Yakima held her. He rocked her for a long time. He felt her heart beating against his. It was a nice feeling. He didn't want it to end.

He pulled away and said, "Keep your chins up, ladies. Just the way you did on the trail. Keep your chin up, keep moving forward. Remember that the three of us will always be good company"—he thumped his chest with his fist—"right here."

He gave the quietly sobbing Annie one last hug, tussled Beth's hair, surprised to find the stout-hearted younger girl shedding a few tears now, as well. He turned away abruptly.

He climbed into the saddle, reined Wolf toward the main trail and booted him into a trot.

He looked back. The girls stood where he'd left them, watching him.

Yakima flung an arm up in a wave then turned his head forward and did not look back again.

Epilogue

A week later, following the directions of Captain Wes Hewitt, whom he'd met at Fort Abercrombie, Yakima stopped Wolf where a secondary trail forked away from the main one. The trail was snow-dusted, for it had turned cold and a light snow had fallen overnight.

Yakima gazed across the dun brown prairie under a cloudy autumn sky, his breath fogging the air before him, toward a small dugout cabin flanked by a sod barn and an unpeeled pole corral in which a couple of swaybacked mules stood together, head to tail.

Smoke issued from the cabin's crooked chimney pipe.

A rusted plow leaned against one side of the corral, nearly buried in the dead, overgrown weeds.

Poverty hung like a blanket over the humble place. From inside the cabin, Yakima heard the sound of a wailing child.

Captain Hewitt had warned Yakima that the Cahill farm wasn't much. Two past droughty years had nearly done in Paul Jr. and his wife, Wynona, as well as their four children, two of which were twins. Cahill wanted to move to Fargo and get a job in a general store or feed barn and build up a stake for a house, but at the moment he couldn't afford to leave.

Yakima pulled his shirt out of his pants and removed the money belt. He held the long, fat snake of the belt up before him. It was satisfyingly heavy and should go a long way in helping the Cahill family fulfill their dreams.

He hung the belt from his saddle horn. Reaching into his shirt pocket, he produced the crumpled envelope containing Paul's letter.

He gazed down at it, running a thumb across it, fondly remembering the man who'd spent so many hours around lonely fires, frantically scribbling the words on the pages.

Yakima smiled and rode forward.

A LOOK AT: ONCE A MARSHAL (BEN STILLMAN BOOK 1)

FROM THE CURRENT KING OF THE VIOLENT, SEXY, HARD-HITTING WESTERN

The Classic Sheriff Ben Stillman Series Begins...

Playing poker, smoking cigarettes, drinking whiskey—retirement was treacherous business for ex-lawman Ben Stillman. The best of life seemed to be past, but then the past came looking for him...

The son of an old friend rides into Ben's life with a plea for justice and a mind for revenge. Up on the Hi-Line in Montana, a rich Englishman is rustling ranchers out of their livelihoods... and their lives. The boy suspects these rustlers have murdered his father, Milk River Bill Harmon, and the law is too crooked to get any straight answers.

But can the worn-out old lawman live up to the legendary lawman the boy has grown to admire?

For fans of William W. Johnstone and George P. Cosmatos's Tombstone, you'll love this first novel in the epic, fast-paced Sheriff Ben Stillman series.

AVAILABLE NOW ON AMAZON

ABOUT THE AUTHOR

Peter Brandvold grew up in the great state of North Dakota in the 1960's and '70s, when television westerns were as popular as shows about hoarders and shark tanks are now, and western paperbacks were as popular as Game of Thrones.

Brandvold watched every western series on television at the time. He grew up riding horses and herding cows on the farms of his grandfather and many friends who owned livestock.

Brandvold's imagination has always lived and will always live in the West. He is the author of over a hundred lightning-fast action westerns under his own name and his pen name, Frank Leslie.

Made in the USA
Monee, IL
05 May 2021

67802990R00157